MY LOVELY FRANKIE
'An achingly heartfelt story about the loves that shape our lives, and the people who show us the beauty of the world'
— *Will Kostakis*

THREE SUMMERS
'Judith Clarke's prose is breathtakingly beautiful and she has the gift of rendering emotions exquisitely'
— *Magpies*

THE WINDS OF HEAVEN
'I was most struck by the deftness, beauty and originality of Clarke's imagery – a wonderful novel, which deserves a wide readership'
— *Bookseller and Publisher*

ONE WHOLE AND PERFECT DAY
'Clarke's sharp, poetic prose evokes each character's inner life with rich and often amusing vibrancy'
— *The Horn Book*

KALPANA'S DREAM
'This novel is a hymn to the importance of imagination in our lives'
— *Australian Book Review*

STARRY NIGHTS
'Clarke has woven a fine tale of grief and mystery – the deft plotting and effective build-up of suspense keep readers guessing about events'
— *Booklist*

WOLF ON THE FOLD
'a beautifully crafted, thoughtful and rewarding book'
— *Viewpoint*

Also by Judith Clarke

Angels Passing By
Night Train
The Lost Day
The Heroic Life of Al Capsella
Al Capsella and the Watchdogs
Al Capsella on Holidays
Friend of My Heart
The Boy on the Lake
Panic Stations
The Ruin of Kevin O'Reilly
Luna Park at Night
Big Night Out
Wolf on the Fold
Starry Nights
Kalpana's Dream
One Whole and Perfect Day
The Winds of Heaven
Three Summers

My Lovely Frankie

JUDITH CLARKE

ALLEN&UNWIN

SYDNEY • MELBOURNE • AUCKLAND • LONDON

First published by Allen & Unwin in 2017

Allen & Unwin
83 Alexander Street
Crows Nest NSW 2065
Australia
Phone: (61 2) 8425 0100
Email: info@allenandunwin.com
Web: www.allenandunwin.com

A Cataloguing-in-Publication entry is available from the National Library of Australia
www.trove.nla.gov.au

ISBN 978 1 76029 633 9

Teachers' notes available from www.allenandunwin.com

'Give me a thousand kisses' is from Poem 5, 'Let us live, my Lesbia, and let us love'
by the poet Gaius Valerius Catullus
'Falling in Love Again' is the English name for a German song composed by Friedrich
Hollaender, with English lyrics by Sammy Lerner, sung by Marlene Dietrich
'Hushabye', traditional song

Cover and text design by Karen Scott Book Design
Cover photo by Shutterstock, papers by The Hungry Jpeg
Set in 10.5/17pt Sabon by Karen Scott Book Design
Printed and bound in Australia in June 2018 by Griffin Press

3 5 7 9 10 8 6 4

MIX
Paper from
responsible sources
FSC® C009448

The paper in this book is FSC® certified.
FSC® promotes environmentally responsible,
socially beneficial and economically viable
management of the world's forests.

For Yask

1. NOW

It's a late summer evening and I'm out on the veranda on the swing seat Miri sent me. *They call them gliders in America,* she wrote. *Like fruit bats, eh? Anyway, I saw it in the window of Montgomery's last time I went into town—they were having a garden display: deckchairs and lounges and these swings, all under a big sign that said 'Summer's Ease', and I pictured you out on the veranda on a warm evening, taking your ease, Tom, dreaming away.'*

Dreaming was underlined. She thinks I do a lot of that. Miri's my cousin, my only cousin, though if I had a hundred of them, she'd still be my favourite. We first met when I was five and she was nine, and straight off, I loved her. I loved the way she looked: the small tanned face and big dark eyes, the springy curls, the sudden amazing smile. I loved the way she moved, always on the point of breaking into a dance. She lived with my Aunty Sarah and Uncle Joe on a property in the north, and when she was leaving us that first time I stood at the barrier with my parents and watched her walking across the tarmac, back very straight, holding fast to Aunty Sarah's hand. When they reached the small plane they turned and waved, then Aunty Sarah went up the steps and Miri followed, still with her back to me; she ran up two steps and then sprang round to wave again (this time, I knew, just for *me*), then two steps more, another turn, another wave, right up to the top, where the hostess grabbed her hand and whisked her out of sight. 'That's a Fokker Friendship,' my father said as the little plane taxied down the runway and rose up into the sky. 'They last forever, just about.'

Like Miri and me. We've lasted. Over the years I've told her most of this story, the one I'm telling now, the story of Frankie, the boy I loved when I was sixteen.

*

Miri's glider arrived in a big flat box, in pieces which you assembled yourself. I've never been much good at that sort of thing, and my neighbour Jim Berry saw me struggling on the veranda and came over to give me a hand. 'There!' he said, when we'd finally got the whole thing together, giving it a small shove with his foot, setting it gently rocking. 'There you go!'

Something about the way he stood there, smiling, rubbing the palms of his big hands down the sides of his jeans, made me think of Frankie. Frankie would have been the kind of man who'd be good at this: good at fitting stuff together and making it go right, making it part of what he called the 'lovely, lovely world'.

The lovely, lovely world. Out here, it's all around me: across the road a group of kids in baggy shorts and big tee-shirts are kicking a ball around the oval; dust and the last smoky sunlight blurs their outlines so they seem soft and cloudy as young ghosts. Dusk is falling, and it's exactly the way Frankie described it to me back at St Finbar's. If I let my mind drift easily, lazily, without actually *trying* to bring him back, sometimes I'll hear his voice as clearly as I hear those young boys over there. It happens now. 'And the dusk,' he's saying, 'the dusk, back where I come from, it's like—it's like—*flour*—' He gives a little whoop of pleasure because he's found the word. 'Flour,' he repeats delightedly, 'you know, when someone's mum's making a cake and she's sifting flour and it falls down over all the stuff in the bowl—that's our dusk in Currawong.'

I look out across my garden. Yes, there's his dusk, falling gently like sooty flour from some enormous sieve—and up there in the sky I can even make out those little green stars he talked about, the colour of new apple leaves, just beginning to show—

*

Frankie lived in this town when he was a boy, in Lisson Street, Currawong, number three. The first time I came looking for him was on the annual leave of my very first posting. I was twenty-four. It was a full eight years since I'd last seen him. I could have come sooner, why didn't I? I could have come when I finished at St Finbar's, or even on one of those summer vacations when I was seventeen, eighteen, nineteen—I know my parents would have given me the money for the fare. I thought of him every day, and yet I waited years.

'Why?' Miri should have asked me when I told her this. 'Why didn't you go sooner? Why did you wait so long?'

She didn't ask because I think she knew the answer. I waited so long because I was afraid. You see, as long as I didn't go, I could think that Frankie was safely there, back with his family in Currawong, perhaps even married to Manda Sutton or some other local girl.

I've always been a fearful kind of person: a sheltered child, a bookish child, a kid who was 'good at school'. I think that's why my father used to take me with him on his doctor's rounds some nights, to get me out into the world, to get me to *see* things. Once I read that fear is a kind of wickedness and I believe that's true. You may not even recognise the fear. That doesn't matter, it takes hold of you just the same, wraps itself round you like a python, paralyses—you're no good to anyone. And it never ends—one fear passes, and then another comes behind it, like the waves of the sea. On the bus to Currawong that first time I started to feel afraid, not that Frankie wouldn't be there, which I think I knew already, but that he *would* be—and I'd knock on his door and he'd open it, and he wouldn't remember me. There'd be a couple of little kids clinging to his legs, and a woman's voice would call out from another room, *Who is it, love?* and he wouldn't know what to reply because he wouldn't recognise this stranger at his door.

Of course, he wasn't there. The Maguires, his family, had left the town by then. Their old house was a big, ramshackle weatherboard; its paint peeling, the front steps half fallen in, weeds growing through. I could see at a glance that no one had lived in it for years. 'No forwarding address,' the woman at the post office told me; the whole family had left years ago, she hadn't known them, it was before her time. Manda Sutton had gone too; she was Manda Cutler now, married with two children, living in another small town. I didn't bother to ask for her address; I knew she wouldn't know where he was. I went back to Lisson Street and knocked on the neighbour's door. He was the only neighbour; the street was short, the mere beginning of a street—beyond those two houses it petered out into vacant lots and then the straw-coloured paddocks began. It was summer and the air above them seemed to glitter.

'Moved off to the city, the whole lot of them,' said the old man who opened the door. He wasn't sure which city. His name was Ted Stormer and he took me inside and sat me down on his sofa and brought me a glass of orange cordial with a big chunk of ice in it. He hadn't known the Maguires all that well, he told me, he'd only been in this house a few months when they'd moved. August it was, he said. August 1950.

1950 was the year Frankie had been at St Finbar's with me. He'd vanished in the very middle of it, on a freezing night towards the end of June. People said he'd run away, and that after a bit he'd go home, though he'd told me his father would throw him out if he did. He could have gone home to say goodbye to his mum and the little kids, even if it was only for a day, before he went off again to find his way in the world. And if he had come back, then Ted Stormer would have been right next door. He might have seen him. The idea of that sighting made my heart race. 'Do you remember a boy called Frankie coming home that winter?' I asked him. 'A tall boy, blond hair, about sixteen—'

Sixteen. The word stopped me in my tracks. At the very sound of it, I saw Frankie beside me, his face lit by that brilliant sickle moon. *Sweet sixteen and never been kissed!* he was saying. *Sweet sixteen and never been kissed!*

That kind of sudden memory can stun you like a blow. Your whole head seems to open wide. It's the vividness of it, the *life*—so the memory seems more real than the actual life you've got in the here and now, the air you're breathing, the place you're in. Ted Stormer's living room wavered and receded; instead I saw the cold grass full of moonlight on the hillside at St Finbar's, I heard Frankie's voice saying sadly, *I wish you had.* I felt the warmth of him, his body close to mine.

'You all right?'

I snapped out of it, looked up. Ted Stormer was standing beside my chair, staring down at me—at my dazzled face, my hand trembling and the ice rattling in my glass. 'You all right?' he asked again.

'It's just the heat.' It should have been a good excuse in Currawong but I could see he didn't buy it. 'I'm okay.' I took a big gulp of orange cordial and he watched me for a few seconds before going back to his chair.

'This Frankie. Good mate of yours, was he?' His rough old voice was gentle.

'Yeah.'

He rubbed at his stubbly jaw and his bright eyes wandered towards the window, where you could see a bit of the Maguires' yard, and a rusting old bicycle lying in the weeds. 'He was sixteen, you said? This mate?'

Sixteen. I waited for Frankie's voice to come again, and the cold moony hillside, but they stayed away. I cleared my throat. 'Yes, he was sixteen. Tall. He had blond hair. You'd have noticed him if he came there that winter.' Everyone noticed Frankie.

'No such thing as winter in this place.' The old man leaned towards me. His big smile was full of delight. 'But 1950— I remember that year because it wasn't long since the wife passed away and I'd just come here and everything sort of— struck. It was very clear, every little thing hit you, know what I mean?'

I did know. 'Yes.'

'Well, I'm thinking hard, and the only boys I remember next door were the twins, Paul and Markie, they were called. Little boys—the only big kid was a girl, had an odd sort of name.'

'Dymphna.'

'That's it. But no Frankie, not that I remember. I never saw any older boy. Not that winter or any time.' He stared down at the carpet. 'Not that I had that much to do with them, mind—just the odd word over the fence, now and again. They pretty much kept to themselves, the Maguires. They went to the church a lot though. You tried the people up there?'

*

'We went to early mass every morning,' Frankie had told me. 'All of us, every morning, even in winter when it was still dark, even when it was raining.'

Back in those days there were still families who did this. I remember waking in the early mornings and hearing their footsteps going past our house, the hushed voices, the occasional soft laugh. It was ordinary life. 'And then, when we got home again,' Frankie went on, 'Dad would do it all over again.'

'Do what?'

'Say the whole mass again. From this little book he had, sort of like a priest. We had to kneel down and say all the responses before we could have breakfast, and we'd be so hungry—sometimes the little kids would cry. And then he'd get angry—'

There was no way you could say that was ordinary. I thought his father sounded spooky. I remember we were walking through the cloisters when he told me this; it was shadowy in there but you could see the sun at the end like a door full of light and I remember glancing at his face to see how he felt about these things he was telling me. I'd thought he looked puzzled, even slightly stricken, as if he was trying to work something out and it wouldn't come, like a problem in maths where you couldn't get the answer however many times you tried. But when we came out into the sunlight of the courtyard he smiled at me and I thought the stricken expression might simply have been in my imagination.

*

When I left Ted Stormer's place that afternoon I went up to the church. The priest was only a few years older than me and he'd trained in New Zealand, so he hadn't been at St Finbar's, and if he guessed I was in the same profession he didn't say anything. His name was Edwin Dunbar and, like the lady at the post office, it turned out the Maguires were before his time too. He gave me some names of older people in his congregation and a few younger ones who might have been at school with Frankie and I wandered round town, asking here and there. Ted Stormer had been right: the Maguires, as a family, had kept pretty much to themselves. No one seemed to have been close to them; no one knew where they'd gone. No forwarding address had been left at the school or the church or the council office. I tracked down a couple of Frankie's old schoolmates and they remembered him all right, though they'd never heard from him after he left for St Finbar's. 'Frankie Maguire? Yeah!!! What's he up to these days, then? Bet he didn't stay long in that place! Drop us a line if you find him, eh?'

*

Forty years after that first visit I came back here to Currawong, this time to stay. A retirement posting, they called it. Miri shook her head when I told her. 'Oh, Tom! Why do you want to bury yourself in that hole, miles from anywhere? No, don't tell me, I know. It's where *he* lived! Now what earthly good is it going to do you to go and live where he used to live? When he was a *child*. Face it, Tom, he's gone from there, he's gone years and years ago. And you know it!'

'Sometimes,' I said, 'when people get older, they come back to see the place where they grew up.'

'You don't believe that. Not about Frankie.'

I said nothing and she stamped her foot, like she used to do when we were kids and argued. Despite the arthritis in her hip, she stamped that foot hard. 'Oh, get a life, Tom!'

Get a life! It's something her grandchildren say, I think.

'I've got one,' I said.

She put her hands on her hips, firmly. She glared at me. 'Tom Rowland! I give up on you!'

She hasn't though. She wouldn't. Not yet.

*

Outside my front fence in Currawong, a can rattles down the street, there are shouts and running feet, the boys from the oval are going home. As they pass beneath the streetlight I see they're about the same age Frankie and I were at St Finbar's, and I think how the life we lived in the seminary would be quite unimaginable to them. That there could be a place where you always felt hungry and where you might get into trouble for giving a piece of bread to another hungry child! For singing a lullabye! A place where it was wrong even to glance at a girl in the street, wrong to look around you at the things of the lovely world. 'Guard your eyes!' Etta's thin voice would call out as we walked in our bleak little crocodile through the streets of Shoreham. 'Guard your eyes!'

Etta.

But I don't want to think of Etta now. Even out here on my own veranda, rocking in Miri's lovely glider, a blackness swarms up when I remember him. I glance at my watch, my father's watch, which he gave me long ago when I was ordained, and I see it's seven-thirty.

Seven-thirty at St Finbar's was the time for rosary. Then we would study in the library till nine-fifteen, after that a brief fast walk around the courtyard—our boots clattering on the paving stones, our breath noisy as a herd of young horses—then prayer and meditation for half an hour. Lights out at ten, when the Great Silence would descend. Every hour, every minute of our days was accounted for—except for those we stole.

Here in Currawong, seven-thirty is the time for my evening walk round to Frankie's old place in Lisson Street. There's no house there now, of course, it was knocked down years before I came here. 'And just as well,' said Miri, 'otherwise you'd have bought it.' Yes, I would have, but by the time I retired all that was left was a stretch of rough grass turning to paddock and a single gnarled rosebush where the front steps used to be.

As I walk past this place my lips start moving, forming silent words. Anyone seeing me would think poor old Father Rowland was mumbling some kind of prayer. They'd be quite wrong—it's a poem I'm saying, my father's favourite, the one he used to get me to read to him when he was dying.

Give me a thousand kisses, then a hundred,
Then another thousand, then a second hundred,
Then yet another thousand, then a hundred...

And so on till the end, and then I head towards home. My place isn't all that far from Frankie's if you go down the back lanes—though I never do. I take the long way, the one Frankie took on that dusky evening when he met Manda Sutton: along the old highway for a bit, across a paddock and down Jellicoe Lane—*the long way down Jellicoe Lane*—until I reach the place beside the cherry trees. The trees are old now, the branches gnarled and dry; they don't bear fruit anymore. You get a little wispy blossom in the spring, nothing like it was in Frankie's time when he told me those trees looked like a row of brides.

'You're a sad old frump, Thomas Rowland,' Miri would say if she saw me standing here, but you know, somehow I don't think I am. A tiny breeze stirs the leaves and a faint delicious perfume trembles in the air. Somewhere water chuckles over pebbles and there are evenings when I'm almost sure I hear a low breathy voice, Manda Sutton's voice, calling from some lost veranda, *Is that you, Frankie Maguire?*

2.

Manda Sutton was the reason Frankie came to St Finbar's. We all had our reasons—he told me about her the very first night we spoke together through the flimsy wall between our rooms. 'It was this thing that happened,' he said simply. 'And then I came here.'

He'd been late getting out of school that afternoon; Sister Josephine had given him a detention for mucking round in class, she'd left him alone to write out his lines and hurried off to the convent next door. 'I'll be back,' she'd warned him. 'Don't you think I won't be, Frankie Maguire! And I wouldn't like to be in your shoes if I find you gone!' When she did come back, long after he'd finished her task, the room was full of shadows and he was gazing out the window at a long caravan of skinny pink clouds and thinking how the weather might turn, not tonight but tomorrow; early in the morning and he'd wake up to that wonderful smell of rain on dusty earth. As she came through the door she was wiping her mouth with a big white hanky and he guessed she'd been having tea with the other sisters and forgotten all about him. 'You may go,' she'd said, folding the hanky back into her pocket. There was a small scattering of crumbs on her bodice and Frankie simply couldn't help himself—'I knew she'd get mad but I had to do it,' he said. He'd pointed to the crumbs. 'You've missed a couple there, Sister.' The look she'd given him was so poisonous it would have dropped the crows dead from the trees and he'd sidled past her quickly and fled. Down at the oval he'd run into Bri Mcphee and Mick Slater kicking a ball round and he'd stopped and had a go with them. And when they'd got sick of it and Bri said, 'Better get on home,' he'd looked round and seen that dusk was falling. 'What's the time?' he'd asked, and Mick had peered at his watch and said, 'Nearly seven.'

Seven. At home they had tea at six. Right on the dot. Always. By now his mum and Dymphna would be washing the dishes in the kitchen. His dad would be sitting in his chair and though it would look like he was reading the paper, Frankie knew better. 'He'd be sitting there waiting for me,' he said. 'I could *see* him—in the good shirt and trousers that he wore to work. He always kept his good clothes on till we'd all gone to bed. You'd never see Dad in his singlet, not like other dads.'

There was a silence then and I thought—it was so long—he'd gone to sleep. 'Frankie?' I wanted to hear the rest of the story.

He wasn't asleep. 'Yeah?'

'What happened then? When you found out it was so late? What happened when you got home?'

'I didn't go home, not right away. It was funny—I knew I was late and he'd be on the warpath and the later I was the worse I'd get. I knew Martha—she's the biggest of the little kids—would be saying, 'Frankie's late again—'

'Telling.'

'Oh no,' he was quick to defend her. 'It wasn't like that. I mean, Martha does tell on people, but it's not because she wants to get them into trouble, not really. It's because she's in the middle, see, between me and Dymphna and the little kids, and no one notices her much. All she wants is—she wants someone to pick her up, that's all. Only she's too big for that.' He went silent again, as though he was thinking about Martha and the rest of the story wasn't important to him anymore. By now it was important to me. 'So what did you do, if you didn't go home?'

'Oh, I did go home, only not just then. I was putting it off, I think. I took the long way down Jellicoe Lane.'

The long way down Jellicoe Lane. There was something musical, almost magical in the way he said those words. They sounded like the title of a song.

In those days there were hardly any houses in Jellicoe Lane, only the Parr's place on the corner and the Sutton's half a mile down, bush in between, and then the stand of cherry trees. It was spring and they were covered in blossom and he stopped in front of them. 'They looked like brides,' he said. He stood there for a long while, gazing at them and then up at the sky which had rosy streaks across it and those soft little greenish stars.

'I started singing,' he told me. 'I couldn't help it. "All Things Bright and Beautiful" it was, like little kids sing.'

That must have been when Manda Sutton heard him. The old Sutton place isn't far behind those cherry trees—half a small paddock, a bit of rough garden, and you're there. It was a warm night, Manda would have been lounging out on the veranda and suddenly there'd be this boy's voice singing through the dusk and it would have sounded like some amazing invitation; she'd have come down the steps and across the yard and over the paddock towards the cherry trees.

'It was such a beautiful night,' said Frankie. 'You could smell the summer coming, you could feel it in the air. I took off my shirt, I wanted to feel that air on my skin—and then I heard this girl's voice coming from behind the cherry trees. "Is that you, Frankie Maguire?" She knew my name! It was Manda Sutton. She came walking out and stood there, right in front of me.'

He knew her, of course, in the way you know most people in a small place like Currawong, unless they keep very much to themselves. She was a few years older than him, long out of school because her mother had died and she had to help her dad at home. He knew the older boys said she'd go with you, go with anyone. For nothing. The way she stood there right in front of him, staring at his bare chest made his face go red. 'I went to pick up my shirt, only she grabbed it, she got it first, she chucked it away and for a moment we were both standing there watching it sailing away, like a big white bird into the trees. She was laughing; she said I didn't need it anyway because it was so warm. She got up so close to me I could feel her breath on my skin, and she kept on talking about how warm it was, and I couldn't get any words out, you know, to answer her. I didn't know what she wanted me to say, I was just standing staring like a kid. She was wearing this really short little dress made of shiny stuff. I think it might have been a petticoat.'

A petticoat. The word sounded strange in my austere little room at St Finbar's. Alien, yet beautiful too, and I felt a strange sharp pang, like wanting something for which you had no name.

'Then she touched me,' said Frankie, and when he said this I felt a little jolt. 'She put out her hand and ran a finger down my chest and it made me shiver all over, and then she laughed and she said it again.'

'Said what?'

'Is that you, Frankie Maguire?'

He'd answered this time. 'Yes, it's me,' he'd said, and she'd taken his hand and the next moment he was walking beside her, his hand closed in her warm fingers, and then they were in a kind of grassy hollow behind the cherry trees and Manda was taking off the shiny dress which might have been a petticoat. He'd never seen a naked girl before. At home he'd never seen any of them, except for the baby, without their clothes. They had to be careful always, his father told them, to hide the body's sin. 'What sin?' Frankie had asked once. 'What sin?' 'He didn't answer me. He said not a word.'

And when Manda was standing in front of him and the little petticoat was gone, he felt a kind of amazement: he'd never have guessed how beautiful she was without it, he'd never have guessed at those sweet white breasts that made his heart hammer and the breath catch in his throat. Or those rounded, gleaming thighs. 'Never,' he said, ferociously, almost. 'Never.'

'Frankie,' she'd said again. 'Frankie Maguire.' And he said the way she spoke his name, so carefully, as if he was someone solid, important even, made him feel strong and unafraid of anyone and he'd fumbled with the button of his grey school trousers, trying not to think of his mum sewing it on for him, sitting at the table in the kitchen, her eyes screwed up to see. His mum said girls like Manda Sutton were bad but it seemed to him she was good, that she was part of everything, the dusk and the cherry trees, the dark smell of earth and the little green stars the colour of new apple leaves. The sweet curves of her body were good in a way those things were good, and she made him feel part of everything too.

Only afterwards, when they were lying together, he felt her body suddenly grow tense. 'There's someone in the lane,' she'd whispered, pushing him off her and sitting up, reaching briskly for her clothes. 'Listen! Hear that?'

Twigs were snapping. Feet crunching roughly through the grass like they didn't care what they flattened.

Manda was up in a flash, pulling the shiny petticoat over her head.

Frankie didn't have time for anything. A thin dark shape,

familiar, burst through the cherry trees. Manda was gone already. A furious voice was shouting.

'It was Dad,' said Frankie. 'He'd got sick of waiting and come out looking for me. I don't know how he found us. We must have been making a lot of noise.'

*

It wouldn't be much of a problem today. It wouldn't even have been a great problem back then, unless Manda Sutton had got pregnant, and she didn't. But Frankie's father was the kind of person my own father used to call a holy savage: someone who enjoyed power in his family because he had little of it elsewhere, who liked to control and punish and believe he was doing it in the name of God. Frankie was beaten three days running and kept inside the house. Manda Sutton was ignored; though if news of a pregnancy had come, he would have been forced to marry her. His father told him he'd offended Heaven. Frankie would wake in the middle of the night and find him standing beside his bed, shouting how Frankie had made the Blessed Virgin weep and plunged a sword into Christ's side and God's face had turned away from him.

Frankie believed him. 'I could *feel* it,' he said. He could feel Heaven itself turning; when he went out into the garden at night and looked up at the sky the stars were dimmed and far away. A thick muddy slime seemed to set hard in his veins. He felt cold all the time. He went to confession and Father Nolan absolved his sin but the coldness was still there. 'I'm sorry,' he said to the statues in the church, to Mary and St Joseph and St Francis and St Patrick, and Jesus hanging above the altar—none of it did any good. He thought he might never get warm again. In the kitchen at home he heard his mum whisper to his dad, 'I'm ashamed to say my prayers.' A mottled flush had spread over her cheeks.

'There!' said his dad triumphantly. 'See what you've done!' Dymphna wouldn't talk to him and Martha and the little ones looked at him with big frightened eyes and pressed themselves against the walls when he walked past. 'When I tried to talk to them they ran away!'

He heard his footsteps sounding hollow on the floors. 'It was the opposite of Manda,' he said. 'She made me feel strong, even if it was only for a bit. They, my family, made me feel I wasn't really there. Like I was no one.'

He went to the church again and knelt in the small side chapel. Jesus on the cross was looking down at him, and Frankie fixed his eyes on the narrow white feet, which were nothing like the broad cracked ones you saw round Currawong. Even without the painted wounds he thought Christ's feet looked piteous and hurt. 'I'm sorry, sorry, sorry,' he whispered, and added in a rush, 'I'd do anything for you. Anything.' He lifted his head and the marble eyes were waiting.

'I'll give my life to you,' he promised, and thought he heard a long, soft sigh.

'So that's how I came here,' he said.

*

Sometimes I think everything that happened came from that spring evening when Frankie was late and took the long way home. If Sister Josephine hadn't kept him in, if his mates hadn't been out there on the oval, if the evening hadn't been so beautiful that he'd suddenly started singing, if Manda Sutton hadn't been out on the veranda and heard—

Then his dad wouldn't have caught him, he wouldn't have come to St Finbar's, I would never have met him. Etta would never have seen him, he would never—Etta's face rises up before me, those pallid cheeks and deep-set eyes, the strange domed shape of his skull—But no, I still don't want to think about Etta. Not yet.

3.

The first time I saw St Finbar's I was seven years old, a long time before I met Frankie. My father was a doctor with a busy practice in a poor suburb of the city. He hadn't much time for holidays, but that year he took a whole week off and the three of us went to the small seaside town of Myall. We stayed in a fibro bungalow at the end of Ocean Street, a mere strip of bright green buffalo grass between us and the beach and sea.

It was lovely. The loveliness rushed over me the minute I woke up: the sea outside our windows and no school, Dad with us all day long, no one to ring or come knocking for him at the door. Every morning after breakfast we'd walk along the beach and over the rocks to the swimming baths. The days were hot and brilliant, the sea a calm sheet of blue on which floated patches of a darker, deeper blue. That colour thrilled me, the way it was so dark and yet full of light. Simply to look at it made me feel rich; it was something to think of at night, before you went to sleep. It made me happy. From the concrete steps above the baths we could see the next little town across the bay, its streets and houses, a long row of Norfolk pines, and above it, high on the headland, something grand: great walls of sandstone, long arched windows, turrets and a tower.

'Is that a castle?'

They looked where I pointed, my dear long-gone parents. They were young then, their faces were flushed with the sun, drops of salt water sparkled in their hair—

'A castle?'

'Where?'

'There!'

'Oh, he means St Finbar's.'

They looked at each other, and then they laughed. It was a special kind of laugh, for them only, I thought.

'What's St Finbar's?'

'It's—it's a school for boys who want to become priests.'

'Like Father Boyle at home?'

'Well, yes.' They smiled at each other.

I stared up at the great building. It must have been a feast day because there was a flag flying bravely from the tower. I'd never seen anything like it outside a picture book. How could it be a school? It was a palace; I couldn't believe old Father Boyle had ever been inside it, he was far too ordinary. I thought kings and queens and knights in armour must live up there behind those thick stone walls. As we walked back across the rocks I kept turning to stare at it, tugging at my mother's hand.

*

Eight years later I decided I wanted to be a priest. My parents thought I'd got the idea from school—I hadn't, it was all my own. I loved my parents, I was happy at home and school, yet this ordinary happiness didn't seem enough for me. I was greedy, I suppose, I wanted more. I wanted to be special, I wanted wonders, glory. I wanted, not to be rich, but richness, the kind of richness I'd sensed in the colour of those floating patches on the sea at Myall, the colour whose name I now knew from our art lessons: indigo. 'Indigo', I would say to myself at night, 'indigo, indigo.' Then, walking home from school one day I suddenly remembered the castle I'd seen on the headland above that sea: the great walls and battlements and the flag flying against the summer sky—and it seemed to me that it might be a place where you could find richness. 'Indigo,' I whispered.

I felt close to God in those days. When I went into church I'd catch my breath as I passed through the heavy wooden doors. It gave me a little rush of joy to set my feet on the worn red carpet of the aisle, close my eyes for a moment and then look up and see everything in its place, all *there*: the glossy brown pews, the white marble altar and the great crucifix above it—and I swear that I could sometimes sense a hand which must surely be God's, stretched tenderly above my head. I never told anyone about that hand; I never told my parents or teachers or Father Boyle. I never told the Bishop in my interview before St Finbar's, I never even told Frankie on that night he shared the story of Manda Sutton with me.

'I should have,' I whisper to myself, 'I should have *told* him.'

I told Miri though. Not then, not when we were young, but much later, when we were both in our fifties, long after Frankie had gone and her husband Chris had died. 'You won't believe this,' I began, a little diffidently, 'but when I was a boy, that time before I went to St Finbar's, I really did think—no, I actually *felt* it—that God's hand was stretched out, just above my head. Protecting me, you know.' I thought she'd smile— Miri was never a believer, or so it seemed to me back then. But the glance she gave me was utterly straight and serious. 'Perhaps it was,' she said.

*

Though they both came from old Catholic families, my parents weren't happy with my plans.

'You'll never have children,' my mother said. 'You'll never have a family of your own, Tom. I can't understand it.'

'I've got a family, I've got you and Dad.'

'We won't always be here, Tom.'

It took me a moment to understand that she meant they would die some day, and when I realised, I had a small feeling of shock, even anger, that they'd leave me in this way. It was I who was leaving them, but I didn't understand this, I didn't understand their unhappiness with my decision. 'You're just scared I'll get like Father Boyle,' I said, trying to make a joke of it. 'You think I'll grab the best chair when I come to visit and expect you to wait on me.'

She tried to smile. I watched her lips curve slowly and then droop down again so sharply that it looked as if some tiny essential muscle had been cut. She touched my cheek lightly and I felt how cold her fingers were.

'You need to consider that you might feel differently in a few years' time,' my father said. 'You've only just turned sixteen.'

I didn't want to consider anything, I was sure. I knew— *then*—I'd always be sure. It was that simple. I wanted to go *now*. Already I felt late—other boys had entered the seminary at twelve or even eleven. I felt panic-struck; it was like being in love when you're too young. It made me desperate, it made me cruel. I screamed at him, 'You can't stop me!'

'I'm not stopping you, I'm simply asking you to *think*.'

'I have. I have thought.'

Sighing, he turned away.

I didn't tell Miri, I don't know why.

'Because you *knew* I'd hate it,' she said later. 'You knew I'd tell you not to go. You knew I'd argue.'

Perhaps. Anyway, I didn't tell her. She heard. I suppose my mother wrote to Aunty Sarah, and Aunty Sarah told Miri. Miri was twenty by then, and engaged to Chris.

Her letter came a few weeks before I left for St Finbar's. It was a card she'd made herself, a simple square of white cardboard, with the single word *DON'T* printed on it fifty times.

I wrote back. *I've made up my mind* I said.

What mind? she replied, on another white card, though

with kisses all around it, like thick blue embroidery. Indigo kisses. I still have that card.

*

Everyone was kind to me in those last weeks before I went to the seminary: the people at church, our neighbours, my father's patients. My godparents Denny and Joseph bought me a present, an anthology of modern poetry with fine gilt-edged pages and a red leather cover with a design of a cornucopia spilling fruits and flowers. 'So you can take all the good things with you,' they said. Denny and Joseph were old friends of my parents from university. They were gay, though the term wasn't in use then. 'They love men instead of women,' my father had explained to me. 'It's the love that counts, Tom.' He looked at me then. He said, 'It isn't wrong, Tom. Being able to love another person: in all your life, that's the most important thing.'

*

Most people seemed happy for me, though occasionally I caught the flicker of another expression beneath the kind words—pity, was it? I didn't understand—how could anyone pity me? My friends at school clapped with the others when Father Boyle made the announcement, though afterwards they seemed almost shy of me, as if my decision had suddenly revealed me to be a different person, someone they hadn't really known, and never would now. When I was with them, they steered clear of the subject of my vocation. Only Jimmy Blewett said something.

He was one of the kids from the old army camp on the edge of our suburb, where the long metal huts, freezing in winter, boiling hot in summer, had been made into housing for poor families. My father sometimes took me there on his rounds. It was a rough place, full of fights and drunks and sobbing; the very walls of the huts seemed to vibrate with a kind of roaring. No matter how late it was, how dark or cold or wet, there'd be little kids playing outside in the mud of the trampled paddock that was their yard. I never once saw Jimmy Blewitt on those visits, but I knew he was there somewhere. I knew he saw me. On that day Father Boyle made the announcement, Jimmy Blewitt came up to me in the school playground. 'Geez, Tom, are you *sure*?' he said. He was always in trouble at school, always in fights, like most of the army camp kids. Once he'd sworn at a teacher—yet when he asked me this question, there was a kind of deep seriousness in his voice that reminded me of my father. Yes, that was it, he was like Dad.

Quickly I said, 'I'm sure.'

He stared at me then. He scanned my face so closely that I began to feel uneasy, as if I was telling some kind of lie. Then he said, 'Tom, it's forever. Every day, every day for*ever.*'

His thick, throaty voice rose on that last word, which he made into two: 'for ever' as if to show how long. And when he did that I knew at once that he'd also thought of going to St Finbar's, of 'entering', as we called it. That he'd thought seriously.

'I know it's forever,' I said brusquely. I wanted the subject closed. I didn't want to talk about it.

Jimmy shook his head, shook the whole of his body, like a big dog coming out from a pond. 'I couldn't do it, me,' he sighed. 'I just couldn't, Tom. I thought about it, I thought and thought, and then, I decided—I decided to *stay out*.' He went quiet then, his head was down, his face was hidden, he was waiting for me to speak.

I didn't want to, I was afraid. He looked up and he saw me. He knew me, that's what I thought. He put out a hand and touched my arm. 'Good luck,' he said. Then he turned and hurried away. I watched him get out of sight, up the hill, and then over it, slowly, like he was thinking all the way.

4.

A few weeks before the new term started my parents took me
to see St Finbar's. Father James showed us round; he was the
Philosophy teacher to the senior classes. He'd gone to school
with my father and when he came to our house he and Dad
would sit in the study for hours, smoking and talking together.
He was shy with my mother. Once when Dad persuaded him
to stay for dinner, she passed him a dessert dish and his hand
shook so much that half an apricot slid out and fell onto the
table right in front of him. His long pale cheeks turned crimson,
he jumped to his feet and cried, 'I'm so sorry, so sorry,' in a
voice that sounded almost heartbroken. 'It's nothing, James,'
said my mother, 'nothing at all.' And she cleaned it up, and
made him sit down again and we went on with our meal as if
nothing had happened. Only it had, I could see it. He liked her.
When he thought no one was watching him he would gaze at
her across the table and his face would remind me of the faces
in *The Adoration of the Magi,* a picture we had on the wall at
school. Then suddenly his expression of adoration—I was sure

of it—would be replaced by a flicker of something like fear, and he'd look down quickly at his plate again.

On that afternoon when we came to look round St Finbar's, he had a guilty, almost flinching manner, as if he thought my parents might suspect my decision had something to do with him. He showed us the chapel and the library and the gloomy refectory where we would have our meals. Then he led us down a long corridor lined with portraits of rectors and bishops and archbishops, up a staircase to the room which would be mine in only a few weeks' time. My father took it in with one swift glance, my mother stood in the doorway for a long time, as if she was learning everything she saw in there by heart: the bare wooden floor, the narrow strip of window high up near the ceiling, the wardrobe on one side of the room and the narrow bed on the other, the small desk with a single straight-backed chair. It seemed to dismay her; she put her hand up to her mouth and all of us looked away—my father and I, and Father James. We couldn't think what to say. When we came downstairs again Father James excused himself—he had a meeting—and we were left to explore the grounds.

We walked through the cloisters and down to the sports fields and the vegetable gardens, past the old dairy and then up the hill and along a path beside the encircling wall. The wall was beginning to crumble in places; stones lay on the ground and there were gaps where you could look down and see the road below, a scattering of holiday cottages and the wrought-iron gates of the school I would come to know as St Brigid's.

We walked in silence, all three of us, until the wall gave way to a dense thicket of lantana and blackberry. Somewhere beyond it you could hear the sea. We turned into a narrow track between the bushes, where the sandy ground was the colour of cement, damp and sticky from a recent rain, and thorny strands of blackberry arched over us in a green tunnel whose walls seemed to close us in. The air was thick and warm and small black flies circled dreamily round our heads.

It was a shock when the green walls gave way suddenly to a vastness of sky and air.

'Careful.' My father pulled me back just in time. The ledge where we stood was a mere shelf of grey sandstone, pitted with small hollows that had caught the rain and spray. Down below us the waves boomed unseen. It was a hot cloudy day, everything was grey, the sullen sea and sky merged seamlessly; we could have been gazing out at nothing. Beside me I felt my mother shiver.

'Let's go back,' she whispered, sounding almost frightened. 'I don't like it here.' She brushed at her skirt, a light summer skirt where the sticky grey sand from the track had gathered along the hem. 'I've never seen sand like that before,' she said. 'It's like cement.'

'Come on.' My father caught hold of her hand.

We were silent on the long drive back. I sensed a kind of expectancy in the car. I felt they were waiting for me to say, 'I've changed my mind. I don't want to go to St Finbar's,' but I didn't say it. I hadn't changed my mind. The gloom of the great seminary, that small bare room, it hadn't been enough. Only the ledge above the sea and that strange vacant horizon had frightened me—but I told myself there was no reason I'd ever go there again. It was a long walk from the seminary. It was probably out of bounds.

That night, when I'd gone to bed, my parents talked together in the study for a long, long time. Finally I heard the door open and my mother's footsteps going slowly down the stairs. I got up and walked along the hall. The study door was closed and a muffled thumping came from inside the room. 'Dad?' I called softly. There was no answer. The thumping sound went on.

I pushed the door open. My father was standing at the window, his back to me, one fist pounding at the sill. There was blood. Only a little bit, but I saw it: drops, thick drops, red blood.

Frightened, I closed the door. I went back to my room and I searched for Miri's card, the one with the embroidery of kisses. When I found it I lay down on my bed and studied those two small words and the indigo kisses until I fell asleep.

It was well after midnight when I woke and went downstairs to get a glass of water. The light was on in the kitchen and I saw Dad sitting at the table and Mum standing beside him, smoothing ointment on his knuckles where he'd grazed them against the sill.

The way he looked at her, the way, meeting his gaze, she smiled at him—they were like a small island of perfect tenderness in that uneasy night.

Give me a thousand kisses, then a hundred,
Then another thousand, then a second hundred

They didn't notice me standing at the door. My parents loved each other.

That night it was two weeks and three days and a night till I would first see Frankie. I know the time exactly because I looked at the hall clock as I left the kitchen and it was five to one. Then I glanced through the window on the landing and the night sky was indigo. I count backwards: it was at morning mass on the Saturday of my first week at St Finbar's that I saw Frankie, so when I left my parents in the kitchen and walked up the stairs to my room it was two weeks and four days, fifteen hours and twenty minutes, give or take a few of those, till I first saw Frankie Maguire.

5.

He was late. Being late was so much a part of him. I have so many images: Frankie running down the staircase at St Finbar's, hair still wet from the shower, cassock flying, its top buttons unfastened, bits of grubby shirt escaping from the collar; tearing round a corner, notebooks slipping from his arms. I'll see a classroom, old Father Beasely at the blackboard writing up his interminable notes, young heads bent, perfect silence except for the scrape of chalk—and then there'll be the sound of big boots clattering along the veranda, and our heads shoot up, and there's his bright face at the door. In these images Etta is always there. He's hidden, you never see him, but the sense of him informs the very air. It's like those picture puzzles in the books Denny and Joseph used to give me when I was little—those small mysterious landscapes where a figure hides inside the lines and shadings: 'Where is Farmer Brown's horse?' 'Where is Dog Toby?' 'Someone is hiding. Someone is there.'

*

To be late for your very first day at St Finbar's was something of an achievement because the arrival of new students was meticulously planned. Mimeographed sheets of instructions arrived through the post at our homes: we were to be at Central Station by seven a.m. on Monday, well in time to catch the Northern Express on platform one at seven-thirty. Three hours into the journey we were to alight at the small town of Nyobie, where a local bus left the station for Shoreham at eleven. On arrival at Shoreham we'd be met by prefects and escorted up the hill to the seminary. On rare occasions a student might miss the train at Central, but there was another slower one at noon, another bus to Shoreham, and he'd arrive late that evening, red-faced and flustered, only a few hours behind the rest of us.

Frankie was four days behind.

He came from a very small place in the west; the nearest railway station was in a larger town sixty miles away. Like many people in those days his family didn't own a car; a neighbouring farmer who chanced to be going that way had given him a lift to catch the train. The farmer had dropped him off at the station an hour early and Frankie had set out to explore the town. Staring hungrily into the window of a cake shop he'd heard the whistle at the level crossing gates, which meant the train was already past the station and on its way to the city. The next one wouldn't come for four days. He had no money, only his ticket and a few coins for the bus ride to Shoreham, and the farmer who'd driven him in was long gone.

He'd camped out in the station waiting room for the first night; the stationmaster found him first thing in the morning, still sound asleep. He'd made him tea and then given him directions to his own house down the road. 'The wife'll look after you,' he'd promised. And she did. Frankie spent three days with the Tooheys, bunking down in the sleepout which had once belonged to their grown-up son, eating big country meals. 'Mrs Toohey made a cream sponge on my last night,' he told me. 'It was this high!' And he showed me the height— a space of about thirty centimetres—between his thin brown hands. The mornings he spent talking with Mrs Toohey, whose children had long grown up and moved away, in the afternoons he wandered round the town. 'Everyone was so *kind* to me,' he said. 'So good. I had a lovely time. People *are* good, mostly. It's only when—' I remember he tailed off then, like you do when you've suddenly remembered something bad. I wanted to ask, 'When what?' but I'd only known him for a few days then, and this, together with a kind of sober thoughtfulness in his expression, made me keep silent.

I'd been terribly homesick that week before he came. I hadn't expected it, I hadn't known about homesickness, I'd never been away before. Everything was strange. Our day began at six, when we got out of bed and stumbled to the bathroom, still half asleep, washed and dressed, fumbling with the buttons of shirts and unfamiliar cassocks, then hurried to the chapel for mass and morning meditation. All day long there were classes and study and sport and prayer, meals in the refectory, work in the gardens—every minute was filled up until lights out at ten p.m. There was no time to think about home, to think of anything—we did stuff, that was all. At lights out I would get into bed and plunge almost instantly into sleep, only to wake an hour later in the middle of the Great Silence, that time between evening prayers and breakfast the next morning, when we were not allowed to speak a word.

This was the time I learned about homesickness: how it was quite simply that, a sickness, a low ache all through you, an anguish for home. I'd turn on my side beneath the grey blankets and the pictures would rush in: I'd see the rooms in my house, each piece of furniture, sofas and chairs and tables and beds and wardrobes. I'd see the pictures on the walls and the pattern on the carpets, a long procession of small lost objects right down to the pots of ferns on the front veranda and the cracked cake of soap beside the laundry tub.

That brown fibre mat outside our back door! At home I'd hardly noticed it, now I would see it over and over. I would remember how it was caramel-coloured in dry weather and chocolate in the rain and how in summer its surface was dry and pleasantly prickly, and I longed with all my heart to be standing on it, to feel those dense rough fibres against my bare soles. And my parents! I would wake from that first dead sleep and feel for the torch I kept beside my pillow, shine it on the face of my watch to find the time, then I'd picture what they would be doing at home: my mother reading in her armchair, my father coming in from a night call, the sharp chink of china on the concrete step as he put out the jug for the milkman. The jug was made of pale green china, and even to picture it brought a pang of loss so sharp I wanted to cry out loud.

I was sick for home. 'Offer it up to Christ,' the teachers at my primary school would have said. I'd heard that phrase so many times and never really thought about what it meant. Now, when I did, it hardly made sense to me. Why would God want pain and suffering offered to him? Why would he like it? Wouldn't he want happiness? Wouldn't he want lovely things?

And then, on my fourth night of homesickness, Frankie arrived. I heard footsteps on the stairs and in the corridor, a door opening, something heavy being dragged across the floor of the room next to mine, the sound of a bright voice exclaiming, 'Is that the *window*?' Someone hushing it. 'Shhh!' The door closed, footsteps hurried down the stairs. I heard my new neighbour sigh, a long tired sigh, so close it startled me. I heard his shoes drop to the floor; as he flung himself onto his bed the wall between us seemed to shudder. I put my hand against it and felt a faint tremor; it was no more than a plywood partition where a larger room had been divided into two. That night I heard the long whisper of my new neighbour's prayers through it, I heard each shift of his body on the bed, I heard him cough once, and then a long silence as if he'd gone to sleep. A few minutes later I heard his voice again, slightly muffled, as if he'd turned his face into the pillow. 'Sorry,' he was saying. 'I'm sorry, sorry, sorry,' and for a moment, before I realised he couldn't possibly know I was there, or that I could hear him,

I thought he was speaking to me. Then he really did fall asleep.

I didn't see him in the morning. His door was closed. I thought perhaps he hadn't heard the bell and was still sleeping, but when I knocked to warn him there was no response. He must have got up early. The same thing happened the next morning and the next. In the evenings I lingered on the stairway, watching the boys come up to their rooms, looking for him—this went on for several days, yet we always seemed to miss each other. I had no real idea what he might look like, though that muffled 'Sorry, sorry, sorry', which he repeated every night, had made me picture him as a pale, smallish boy, narrow-faced, with dark hair and big dark eyes, and in the next few days I looked around the refectory and my classes for a new boy like this. It was impossible to find him because most of the boys were new to me, and so many were small and sallow and dark-haired. Yet though I never saw him, I had a feeling of closeness because every night I heard that 'Sorry, sorry, sorry' and those whispered, hasty prayers, and the soft breathing of his sleep, as close to me as if his head was on the pillow next to mine. Once I heard him wake from a nightmare and cry out, 'No, no. No! I didn't do it, Dad!' His voice shook with terror.

Three whole days and a night passed before I finally saw him. It was in the chapel. Mass had ended and we were walking slowly towards the doors when there was a sudden hold-up to our procession. Halfway down the aisle a boy had stopped. He stood very still, his face lifted towards a high window where a pane of opaque glass had been opened and a strip of bright blue sky was shining, and the branches of a gum tree tossing in the breeze. I knew him at once, though physically he was nothing like the boy I'd imagined. He wasn't small and dark and sad-eyed, he was tall and big-boned, his skin tanned, his hair that rich buttery blond that is almost golden brown. He swung his arm gaily towards the window, inviting us all to look up and share that blue sky and the glittering, dancing leaves. Some boys did look, others shuffled uneasily and kept their eyes down, for we were not supposed to stop and gaze about us, to be distracted by the things of the ordinary world. One boy—it was Bri Tobin, though I didn't know him then—looked up and smiled in sheer delight, then his face turned pure bright red and he lowered his head again, and I was reminded of the way Father James would sneak a glance at my mother across our dinner table and then look away again quickly as if it was a sin. Then, in the shadows by the doorway, someone moved, and a voice called out, 'Guard your eyes!'

It was Etta. The shadows hid him, yet that thin reedy voice was distinctive. I knew it from our mealtimes, when he stood to make the announcements from the senior table. Already in those first few days I'd heard the rumours about him: he was the head prefect, and he never let you off the smallest thing, not even on bush picnic days. Students whispered his name, looking over their shoulders—they said he had a thousand eyes, like a fly. They made him sound dangerous and sticky, like a creature waiting in a web.

John Rushall had warned me about him. John was a senior student who'd once gone to my old school. His mother worked in our local library; she was a friend of my mother's and I suspected John had been asked to keep an eye on me. He told me the same things the others had, that Etta never let you off, and that if you got into his bad books he'd never let you go. 'His real name's Brian Cooley,' John had told me, 'but everyone calls him Etta.'

'Etta? What kind of name is that?'

'No one knows. He just came with it, from primary school.'

Years later, at a conference, I asked my friend Vin Taylor about that nickname. Vin had been with Etta at primary school. 'No one at St Finbar's seemed to know what it meant,' I said. 'Though it suited him, somehow.'

'Oh yes,' said Vin. 'It suited him all right.'

'How do you mean?'

'Spell it backwards.'

I did. 'A-t-t-e. Atte?'

'No, no,' said Vin. 'Not Etta, not the girl's name. It's Etah. Try that.'

I tried it. H-a-t-e. It chilled my blood to think that little kids could sense that in him, when they were all so young.

There were bishops in his family, John Rushall had told me. Not just one bishop, like some of us had, but several. 'He'll be one himself one day, you can bet on it, that's why he's here. He's ambitious, watch out for him.'

'Guard your eyes!' that reedy voice called out again. Frankie didn't seem to hear it, his whole attention was fixed on the window, on the waving branches and shining leaves and now a single magpie which flew down, settled on a branch, threw back its small gleaming head and trilled out a long gurgling note. 'Oh, I love that!' exclaimed Frankie, smiling round at us all.

'Guard your eyes!'

This time Frankie heard. He turned from the window and moved into line and as he did our eyes met and I caught my breath, like I used to do when I entered the old church at home. It was the briefest of contacts; in a moment he'd turned and begun to hurry down towards the door and I could see only the back of his head, that thick blondish hair which had a dull gleam like satin ribbon. You wanted to touch it. I must have been staring because the reedy voice rang out, and this time it was directed at me: 'Guard your eyes!'

6.

A few days later I was on my way to morning classes when a prefect handed me a message from Father James. For a moment, hearing the familiar name, unfolding the note and finding the spiky handwriting I'd seen so often on letters lying on the table in our hall, I was afraid that something had happened back home. I think the loneliness and homesickness of that first week had got to me, made me feel the world was an uncertain and dangerous place. I no longer had the sense of God's hand stretched protectively above my head; it wasn't there, and sometimes at night I worried that it never had been. That I'd made it up.

The message turned out to have nothing to do with my family. Surprisingly, it was about Frankie. He had an abscessed tooth and Father James had chosen me to accompany him down to the dentist in Shoreham. The appointment was for four o'clock and I was to meet Frankie at the main gates at three-fifteen. We were excused afternoon study and would be expected back for Benediction at six-fifteen.

When I arrived at the gates at ten past three, Frankie was already waiting. Though we still hadn't really met or even spoken to each other, his face lit when he saw me coming, as if I was his oldest friend. Frankie *liked* people; this was how he was with almost everyone—for him, they were part of the loveliness of the world. 'You're Tom,' he said, and I remember feeling a little thrill of pleasure that he knew my name, even though I realised Father James would probably have told it to him. 'You've got the room next to mine,' he went on. 'I can—' He gave a little gasp as the cold air struck his mouth, and I saw how one side of his jaw was swollen. It must have hurt badly, because for a moment he closed his eyes. 'Don't try and talk,' I said, and we started down the road in silence, but at the first bend, where the road dropped and there was a high bank which protected us a little from the wind, he began to talk again. 'I've never been to a dentist before,' he confided.

'You haven't?'

'There wasn't one where we lived.' He spoke in the past tense, like most of us did now when we talked about our homes, even the little kids in the dormitory upstairs, though some of them were still of an age when—if no one was looking—they might have let their mother hold their hand.

The only boy I knew who didn't talk about his home in this way was Tim Vesey, who had a room on my floor, on the other side of the stairs. He could still *see* his house; it was on the opposite headland, across the bay. I'd noticed him several times standing at the window on the first floor landing; once he'd beckoned me over and pointed the house out to me. You could see the back of it quite clearly, even the clothes line in the middle of the long back yard. 'I saw Mum yesterday,' he'd told me, 'hanging out the clothes.'

'Oh!' I couldn't quite believe him. To see your *mother*. Hanging out the clothes—being ordinary—it seemed somehow impossible.

'All right! Don't believe me,' said Tim Vesey angrily.

'I believe you,' I said. 'It's just hard to, in this place. You know?'

He nodded. 'Thanks,' he said, and ran away up the stairs.

'From where we lived,' said Frankie, 'the nearest dentist was a hundred miles.'

'A hundred *miles*!'

'Yes.'

'What did you do if you got toothache?'

'Waited till it went away.' He winced again. 'I never had one like this, but.'

I thought he might want to know if the dentist hurt; instead it turned out he was worried the college would send a bill to his father. There wasn't much money for extra things like that at home, he confided; there were a lot of them and his dad would blow his top if an unexpected bill arrived. '*Really* blow his top,' he added with a little shudder, and I remembered how I'd heard him wake from a nightmare shouting, 'No, no. No! I didn't do it, Dad!'

'You can't help it if you get toothache,' I said. 'Anyway, I think the dentist here would treat you for free.'

'Why? Why would he do it for free?'

'Well, because we come from there.' I turned and pointed back towards the seminary, and as I did I thought I saw a flash of movement in the big trees beside the gates, as if someone had been hiding there and quickly moved away. I couldn't be sure though, because the wind unsettled everything.

'And so he wouldn't send Dad a bill?' asked Frankie.

'I don't think so.'

Frankie studied the seminary for a moment, thoughtfully.

'Do you like it?' he asked me. 'This place? Being here?'

I didn't know what to say. It was all too complicated. Sometimes I thought I hated the place, at others, in chapel, caught up in the beautiful words of the liturgy, I loved it. 'I haven't made up my mind,' I said.

He smiled at me. 'It's hard.' It was then that I noticed his eyes. They were that same mysterious colour as the dark blue patches I'd seen floating on the sea that long-ago day at the sea-baths in Myall. Indigo. To gaze into Frankie's eyes gave me that same feeling of richness I'd had back then.

'Oh, look!' He was pointing upwards. A hawk had appeared there, hovering so low you could see the individual feathers, the patterns they made, the way they interleaved. It rose and wheeled away into the sky. 'Did you see him?' His voice trembled with a kind of urgency. 'Did you?'

'Yes,' I said, and he flashed me a look of triumph, as if it was the greatest joy to him that something so beautiful could be there, in the world, with him.

*

The dentist's surgery was in a side street behind the shopping centre. I waited on the front steps while Frankie went inside. It was wonderful simply to sit there and watch the people go by in the street, ordinary people—a postman on his bicycle, an old man walking his dog, two ladies about my mother's age with shopping baskets on their arms. Ordinary people. 'Externs' our teachers called them—the term meant anyone who wasn't a priest or a student priest, anyone who was 'outside'. When I'd first heard the word it had given me a prickly, irritable feeling, and late at night, when I woke up and thought about home, it made me really angry. My parents were externs too. I wanted to run to Father James' room, bang on his door and shout, 'Why do you go and visit my parents, then, if they're *externs*?'

'Tom!'

Frankie was on the veranda. 'Tom, look!'

I jumped up from the steps. He was holding out his hand and in the centre of his palm lay the larger part of a back tooth, its root long and gleaming. He lifted it between two fingers. 'Look, it's an actual *piece* of me!'

I loved the way he spoke, as if I was an old friend, as if he'd known me all his life. Behind him the dentist and the nurse stood smiling. You could see from their faces how they liked him too. Everyone liked Frankie—I think it was the brightness in him, the way his long, rather bony face would light up when something pleased him. The brightness was in his voice, too—

– 48 –

people turned their heads when they heard it, it made you think of light.

'It didn't hurt at all!' He took a grubby hanky from his pocket and began to wrap the tooth inside it, carefully. 'I'm going to keep it for always! I'm going to show it to my kids!'

When he said this, the smiles left the faces of his two new friends. The nurse looked almost tearful, for a moment I thought she was going to cry, and there was a flash of something very much like anger in the dentist's eyes, an anger that wasn't for Frankie, but for the long black cassock he was wearing. At the time I didn't really understand that there were people who felt angry at the way young boys were gathered into the priesthood before they were old enough to know what they would lose. All the same, I had a sudden vivid flash of my father's fist pounding on the sill that night we came back from our visit to the seminary, and I remembered my mother saying, 'You'll never have a wife, a family.' And though the idea of having a family still didn't seem important for me, I could see it at once in relation to Frankie. It was so easy to imagine him with little kids, and I guessed this was what the nurse was thinking too. She went over and kissed him. He was so happy, then! He put his hands up to his cheek and laughed. 'Good luck, Frankie,' she said.

Outside in the street, he caught at my sleeve. 'Can we go that way?' He was pointing to a narrow lane across the road. At the end of it was a blue glimpse of ocean behind a row of Norfolk pines.

'I've never seen the sea before.'

'You haven't? What about when you came? You know, when you got off the bus in Shoreham?'

'It was dark. And I didn't know which way to go; it was hard enough finding how to get to St Finbar's. When someone finally told me the way I was so tired I just went straight there.' He stared longingly down the lane. 'None of us have seen the sea in my family, except for Mum, when she was little.'

I looked at my watch. Frankie's appointment hadn't taken very long and there was plenty of time for a detour to the beach and watch the waves coming in, so we crossed the road and began to walk down the lane. It was a windy day but the town wind was different from the one we knew up on our headland. The wind up there was like a savage, especially at night, shrieking across the open spaces, rattling at the windows, beating at the walls. The wind down here was gentler; it was like a happy child tearing about the streets and gardens, tugging at our cassocks, pulling at our hair. When we reached the end of the lane a great cloud of sea mist came tumbling all around us. Frankie batted at it with his fists, laughing. 'What is this stuff?' he yelled. 'What *is* it?'

'It's spray, from the sea.' A gust of wind rushed down the Esplanade and the mist fell back like curtains from a window and showed the sea, breakers rolling in, great glossy ones with the spray flying off them like banners. 'Look, Frankie, look!'

He'd been whirling round like a little kid, his arms stretched wide, now he stopped and stared. His arms fell to his sides, beneath the tan his face paled with a kind of happy shock. 'Is that—it's—' he yelled it out, 'the sea, the sea! The sea!' and soon I was yelling it too. 'The sea! The sea! The sea!'

'Come on!'

We forgot all about being students from St Finbar's. We tore across the road. We didn't bother with the steps, hurling ourselves from the low wall onto the sand, pounding down the beach towards the water. Frankie was faster than me, he reached the edge before I was halfway down, and when I caught up with him he was standing perfectly still, absorbed, entranced, his eyes fixed on the blue line of the horizon and the white crests of the waves rolling in and spilling up the sand. Despite all the running, his face was still oddly pale, and suddenly he closed his eyes, like he'd done when we were coming down the hill and the wind had struck his jaw.

'Are you okay?'

'I'm *fine*!' Those glorious eyes opened, he turned to me. 'Thank you,' he said.

'What for?'

'For *this*.' He waved towards the sea. 'For showing me!'

'But you would have seen it anyway.'

'Not today. Not *now*! Not this very, very minute. Sometimes I think that's all that matters.' He tore at the laces of his boots, pulled them off and slung them round his neck.

'What's all that matters?' I pulled off my own boots and let the little waves run over my feet. They were warm.

'This very minute. This!' He waved towards the sea again.

'The lovely, lovely world. Oh, let's *go*!' And off he went, racing along the tideline, and I ran after him and we yelled and shouted to the sea and the sky as if there really was only this very minute to be happy in. Sometimes we'd stop for breath and then Frankie would study the lacy edges of the waves or pick up a string of seaweed and sniff at it, or turn a shell or smooth stone over and over in his hand. Or he'd simply stand silently and look out at the vast expanse of sea and the glossy waves rolling in. 'And they come in, and come in and come in,' he whispered, 'on and on and on—'

Somewhere over in the town a clock struck the half-hour. Half-past five. It was time to go. With a great regretful sigh and a sudden shake of his head he turned from it all and we made our way back up the sand, struggled into our boots and set off down the Esplanade and the narrow streets which would take us back to St Finbar's. We were almost at the turn-off to the seminary when something happened on the other side of the street. A long crocodile of girls emerged from the gateway of St Brigid's. They wore blue tunics and blazers, black stockings and panamas with a blue stripe around the brim. Four teachers, nuns in black habits, escorted them, two in front and two behind. The teachers ignored us, though there were glances and giggles from the girls. I lowered my head and walked on fast; it was a few minutes before I realised I was walking alone, and when I looked round I saw that Frankie had stopped and was staring across at the girls. As I began to hurry back, a girl halfway along the crocodile turned to look at him, a girl with laughing eyes and heavy black curls tumbling from beneath her hat. She smiled at Frankie and when he saw that smile he took a step towards her, simply walked out into the road like any ordinary boy who'd seen a girl who looked like she might fancy him. I could see he'd totally forgotten the other girls were there, staring, and the teachers, and the looming bulk of our seminary up there on the hill. The girl kept on smiling and Frankie went on walking until he was right in the centre of the road. There was a hush, a stillness—perhaps I imagined it but I don't think so. You could hear the clap of Frankie's boots on the tarred surface of the road, and a long way off the sound of the sea—the long slow wash of it against the shore. Then one of the teachers called, 'Eyes front, please!' and the dark-haired girl turned away from Frankie and skipped into line and the crocodile walked on; one of the teachers shooting a brief, startled glance at Frankie, who stood there in the middle of the road, staring after them. A single car appeared from one of the holiday cottages and edged slowly round him before driving on towards the town. Frankie barely noticed it.

I walked across to him. 'Frankie?'

He swung round. He was fizzing with excitement, his eyes filled with light. 'Did you see her? That girl? The one with the black curls? Did you see how she was smiling at me? I'm in *love* with her! Oh, *love*!' He sang the word out loud and I felt suddenly afraid, as if somebody was watching. We were not allowed to love, unless it was God we loved. Human love was marred by lust, and sex was sin; we were not allowed even to look at girls we passed in the street. One day we would make our vows of celibacy.

'Tom? Did you see her?'

'Yes, but—'

'She's beautiful,' he whispered. Another car edged round us. I touched his shoulder. 'Come on, or we'll get run over.' I steered him back to the footpath and the second we got there he stopped and looked back down the road for the girls. They were turning the corner towards the town, the dark-haired one already out of sight.

It was then I saw Etta. He was close. I had never seen him so close before and I couldn't take my eyes from him: the pallid face with its tiny snub nose and little crimped baby's mouth, the eyes so deep-set they were hardly more than a watery gleam. He was neither tall nor short, there was nothing remarkable about him except for his head—it seemed too big for his body and its strange domed shape was emphasised by the way his hair was cut, shorn so close you could see the pinkish scalp beneath. I was reminded of photographs of half-formed babies I'd seen in my father's medical books; Etta looked to me like something that might need protection from the light.

He was standing in front of a small chemist's shop. He was all by himself and for a confused moment I wondered what he was doing there; it didn't cross my mind till later that he might have been following us, that the dark movement I'd seen earlier in the trees by the seminary gates could have been him. When we'd passed the chemist's shop he must have been inside—had he come out in time to see Frankie walk across to the girl? Had he heard him saying, 'I'm in love with her!'?

Of course he had. He was close enough to have heard every word, and there was a tautness to his spindly body that made me sure he'd seen it all. And that was bad. I knew Frankie's small, eager encounter with the girl—no more than a smile and a few steps across a road, an excited exclamation—was of a different order to any other small breaches of rules we might have committed today: running in public, shouting, wasting our time at the beach. I thought it might even be the sort of thing for which you could be asked, or told, to leave the seminary. To be expelled, to be found unworthy and thrown out was almost the worst that could happen at St Finbar's. There was only one thing worse, and that was leaving of your own accord: no one ever spoke of those boys, it was as if they'd disappeared from the earth. They were the lowest of the low. 'You may count your life a success,' the Rector had told us on our first day, 'if on your coffin the title "Father" is inscribed.' I knew at once I didn't want Frankie to leave. I wanted him to stay. I wanted him to be near me. I needed him there. I didn't ask myself why.

It was then the fear began, the fear about losing him. It would go on for as long as I knew him, changing, growing, lightening a little, then darkening again, always there, constant as the hum of blood in my ears. In that first moment it was like a person standing outside your house, you haven't heard him coming yet already his hand is lifted to knock on your door.

For a split second I had the mad idea of going up to Etta, telling him some story (that the girl was a cousin?), pleading, even though I knew it would be no use—there was no cousin, they would find that out soon enough. I stood there, paralysed, while Etta geared himself up—or so I thought—to walk across to Frankie, seize his shoulder, tell him he was on report and march the pair of us straight up the hill to St Finbar's and the Rector's office.

Yet he did none of these things. Like me he simply stood there, his eyes fixed on Frankie, a gaze so intent that I could almost see the line of it drawn between them through the air. It made me shiver.

Frankie began to turn towards me and I stepped in front of him, obscuring his line of vision so he couldn't see Etta. If fear is a kind of wickedness then that is where my wickedness began, because I said nothing about Etta. I thought if I did it would make things worse; it was possible, even likely, that Frankie would confront him. He was fearless. That was the great difference between Frankie and me. He was afraid of no one except his father, from whom he so deeply wanted love. To someone like Etta, he might say anything.

'Come on,' I said. 'We'd better get going or we'll be late.' He came with me easily; the girl had gone. 'I don't think I can stand it if I don't see her again,' he said, and I half expected quick footsteps behind us, and Etta's reedy voice crying out, 'Stop, you boys!' There was nothing. I started running, and then Frankie was running too and he didn't say anything more about the girl. As we reached the turn-off to St Finbar's, I glanced back over my shoulder, quickly. The pavement outside the chemist's shop was empty. Etta had gone.

7.

Nothing happened. There was no summons to the Rector when we got back to the seminary, nothing all evening long.

Etta had returned from Shoreham, I saw him at dinner, seated at the seniors' table, calmly eating his meal. He never once looked in Frankie's direction, or in mine. We didn't sit together—that kind of easy arrangement between friends wasn't possible at St Finbar's, where each of us had our allotted places for meals and classes, study and chapel.

Announcements were made before dinner began; I'd expected our summons to be amongst them. When it wasn't, I thought that perhaps the Rector hadn't had time to speak to Etta; and then I expected it to come after evening study, and then after rosary, then last thing after night prayers, and when there was still nothing, I thought it would come in the morning after breakfast when more announcements were made.

I should have warned Frankie, of course, so he'd know Etta had seen him down in Shoreham and be prepared. But I had a feeling that if I mentioned Etta to him it would be like pressing the button on some dreadful mechanism which could never be stopped in time. When I thought of the way Etta's gaze, fixed on him, had seemed like a line drawn between them through the air, I felt a strange pricking sensation. Much later, when I told this to Miri, she quoted to me the famous words of the second witch in *Macbeth*: *By the pricking of my thumbs, something wicked this way comes.* And yes, it was like that.

Lying in my bed that night I heard Frankie wake next door. It was surely the perfect time to warn him; we could talk through that thin partition as easily as if we were in the same room. There'd be no one to hear us, even in the middle of the Great Silence. Our rooms were the last ones in that corridor; on the other side of mine was the landing and stairway, then the bathroom—it was only past the bathroom that the rooms began again, a row of them, exactly like my own. Occasionally you would hear someone going to the bathroom, and once I'd heard footsteps on the landing—I'd guessed they were Tim Vesey's, going to look out of the window at his house across the bay. He'd told me he liked to watch the lights go out in his old home, first of all the living room, then the bathroom, then the bedrooms—'so then I know they're all in bed,' he'd said. 'And safe.' Even if he heard Frankie and me talking together, I knew Tim Vesey wouldn't tell.

'Frankie?'

'Tom!' His bed creaked as he moved up closer to the wall. 'Tom, guess what! I dreamed about her! I dreamed about that girl down in Shoreham. You know?'

I swallowed. 'Yes, but—' I was going to warn him then, I swear it. Only he was so excited, so happy—the words flew from him. 'Oh, nothing happened. We didn't do anything—in the dream, I mean. She just turned round and smiled at me, like she did down in Shoreham. Did you see?'

'Yes. Frankie, there's something—'

'She's beautiful. Did you see her *hair*—I loved the way it sort of *swung* when she turned. It was so soft and thick! You could almost feel it, just by looking—like it was in your hands, all soft and alive.' He gave a long, happy sigh. 'She reminded me a bit of Manda—'

'Manda?'

It was then he told me the story of Manda Sutton. Right then, when we'd only really met that afternoon, he told me how he'd had sex with a girl. Casual sex between young people wasn't as common in those days, and when it occurred it was kept secret unless there was a pregnancy, and even then it wasn't talked about. There were boys at St Finbar's who would never have spoken to Frankie again if he'd told them about Manda Sutton. There were boys who'd never been told anything about sex, who didn't know what was happening to them when they had their first erection, their first wet dream. They kept quiet, they kept it to themselves, and some of them would have thought they were monsters, or amongst the damned. Looking back, I think that Etta would have been like this. He was clever, and if a child was clever in those days he was often skipped past grades in primary school and could be in sixth class when he was only nine. People said Etta was barely ten when he entered St Finbar's. We saw his parents once, Frankie and I, through the window of the library; they were pale and proud and pious, the very pattern of well-off respectability—fearful people, I think now. Etta wouldn't have been told a thing.

I lay there that night and listened to Frankie's story, to that bright, untroubled voice which made me think of light. I heard about that spring evening when he'd been kept in and had taken the long way home because he was scared of his father, *the long way down Jellicoe Lane*. The images crept inside my heart and stayed: the dusk that was like sooty flour falling from an enormous sieve, the bridal cherry trees, the little green stars the colour of new apple leaves. I heard how he'd taken his shirt off to feel the warm air on his skin, how he'd started singing, and how Manda Sutton had heard him and walked out through the trees. 'We made love,' he said simply, as if he was speaking in these modern days and not in that narrow time in the middle of the last century, when for boys from his kind of family, sex was only for marriage. I heard how his dad had found out and punished him, and how he'd come to St Finbar's because he'd 'offended Heaven' and wanted to make up for being bad.

Except it hadn't felt bad, he said, 'it didn't feel bad, Tom, what we did—I don't think—' His voice tailed away into a sleepy murmur, in which I heard faintly the single word 'good'.

For a long while after he'd gone to sleep those images went round and round inside my head: the smoky dusk and the trees and stars and Frankie standing with his shirt off, singing 'All Things Bright and Beautiful'. *He* was bright and beautiful, I thought. And Manda Sutton in her shiny petticoat, coming through the trees—she was the reason he'd come here, so I should have felt grateful to her. Only I couldn't. I heard her breathy voice saying, *Is that you, Frankie Maguire?* and I heard the rough crunch of Mr Maguire's footsteps over the sticks and stones. I had never seen Frankie's father, I would never see him, and yet I felt a kind of loathing for him. Beating children was fairly common in those days, but I couldn't bear that Maguire should take his belt to Frankie. 'Three mornings running,' Frankie had said. 'Before he went off to work. And you wouldn't believe it, but he never got a spot of blood on his clean shirt.' Blood. It horrified me. And the casual way Frankie said it, as if it wasn't important that his father should treat him this way. When I thought of Maguire's belt coming down on Frankie's legs, his poor back, I felt sick with fury; my own skin seemed to burn. I wanted to cry out.

Of course there was more to my feelings about the story than my loathing for Mr Maguire. I felt jealous and confused. I say jealous, yet I wasn't sure what I was jealous about: it wasn't that I envied Frankie having sex with Manda Sutton, it wasn't that. I didn't want to have sex with Manda or even the beautiful dark-haired girl down in Shoreham. Yet jealousy was there, fierce and sharp; I recognised it right away, like a needle pushed into a nerve, even though I'd never felt it before. And when I thought of Manda taking Frankie's hand and leading him through the trees, a longing spread all through me. I felt weak and soft. Was it the landscape I envied, the beautiful evening on the edge of spring, as if I wanted to be with Frankie *there:* in Jellicoe Lane beside the cherry trees, with the warm breeze promising summer and the sooty dusk falling and the little green stars beginning to show in the sky. Was that it? Was that what I wanted? I didn't know.

These days I can go to Jellicoe Lane any evening I choose, I can stand in the dusk beneath those trees, I can look up and see the little green stars. Only Frankie isn't there.

8.

When Etta stood to make the announcements at breakfast I still hadn't been able to warn Frankie. Though I'd woken early, I could tell from the silence behind the wall that he wasn't in his room, nor could I find him in the bathroom. I realised that I'd only ever seen him once in the early mornings, on that day after I'd first recognised him in the chapel, and then he'd been hurrying up the stairs, not down them like the rest of us. His face had been flushed, he'd looked happy, his hair and cassock were damp, as if he'd been out walking in the rain, though the sun had been shining outside.

When I reached the refectory Frankie was there in his place. It was too late to say anything to him; at the head of the prefects' table Etta was getting to his feet, the sheet of announcements ready in his hand. In the few seconds of silence before he spoke I noticed how small his hands were, no bigger than a child's, and his feet were small too, and everything about him was immaculate—his cassock looked freshly washed and ironed, and his small polished boots shone almost fiercely beneath its hem. There was something of the creature about him. He reminded me of those animals dressed in neat human clothing you see in kids' picture books: Mr Stoat or Mr Vole.

He read the announcements and there was no summons for Frankie, no summons for me. A couple of kids whose names had been called got up and sidled quickly to the doorway, the passage that led to the offices of the Rector and the Dean of Discipline. I should have felt relieved, and I was—yet I felt apprehensive too. Etta had seen us down in Shoreham, he'd probably seen us on the beach, boots off, yelling, mucking round. He'd seen Frankie walk across to the dark-haired girl— if the teacher hadn't called out Frankie might even have touched her. I'd noticed on the beach how he liked touching, smoothing the shape of a shell or a sea-berry, letting the sand trickle slowly through his fingers, as if to feel each grain. And Etta had surely heard him cry out, 'I'm in love with her! Oh, love!'

If it had been anyone else I could have understood Etta's silence. If it had been John Rushall's friend Simon Barber, for instance, I think he'd have figured how Frankie was new, a friendly boy from the country who might have forgotten in the sudden freedom of an afternoon outside that he was a novice from St Finbar's who wasn't supposed to have anything to do with girls. That it hadn't sunk in yet. Simon Barber would have gone up to Frankie and given him a warning; he wouldn't have reported him. He'd have let him off.

Etta wasn't like that. Everyone said that Etta never let anyone off, and that was what worried me. It was more than worry, it was like I'd had a whiff of something bad, something wrong. My thumbs pricked. On the way to my first class I saw John Rushall standing on the library veranda and I went up to him.

'Can I ask you something?'

'Sure.' He smiled at me. He had a broad, clear face where nothing seemed hidden and you felt it wouldn't ever be, that messes and secrets simply weren't part of him. My father liked him; my mother said he was a brave, reliable boy.

'It's about, um, about Etta.'

'Etta.' The smile didn't vanish exactly, though it seemed to blur a little.

'You know how everyone says he never lets you off anything?'

He nodded.

'Well, what if he does let you off? What if some kid does something against the rules, and Etta *sees* him, and then he doesn't report it, he doesn't do anything?'

He thought for a moment. 'Big or small? This thing the kid does that's against the rules?'

It sounded an easy enough question, yet I found it hard to answer. When I pictured Frankie walking across the road to the girl, the first thing that struck me was how *right* he'd looked, as if he was doing exactly what he was meant to do. A beautiful girl turns round and smiles at a boy and he smiles back and takes a few steps towards her—what was wrong with that? It was good, wasn't it? And surely it's unkind to ignore another person smiling at you. Except when you turned it round the way Etta would see it, in terms of those rules set out in the little green book we carried in the pocket of our cassocks, then it was wrong. It was a big wrong. It was lust and the girl was an occasion of sin. 'It depends,' I said.

'On what?'

'On what world you're in. If you're outside, if you aren't at St Finbar's, then it's nothing. It's just normal. If you're here, then it's wrong, it's big, or—someone could make it seem big.'

'And he hasn't? We're talking about Etta here?' He lowered his voice and when I looked round I saw that without my noticing, we'd moved to the end of the veranda where an ivy-covered trellis hid us from anyone passing in the courtyard. 'He hasn't said anything to this kid? Hasn't reported him?'

'No. Why wouldn't he? Why would he let it go?'

He frowned slightly. Without his usual smile, his face looked sad and I remembered how he'd lost his father in the war. When I was little my mother used to take me to the library where his mother worked, and if school was out you'd see John at the back of the space behind the counter, reading, sitting very quiet on a chair.

'Why would Etta let it go?' I asked again.

'Because whatever this boy's done, it's not big enough,' he said at last, mysteriously to me.

'How do you mean?'

He spread his hands. 'It's this way: if he's got this kid in his sights, then he's probably waiting.'

'Waiting? What for?'

'For him to do something bad enough to get chucked out.'

'Chucked out! Why would he want to get some kid he doesn't even know chucked out?'

An odd expression flickered across that broad, open face: it was like he knew the answer, only he wasn't sure whether to tell me, whether I'd understand. He considered me for a moment and I could tell this made him even more doubtful. I was small for my age as well as young for it. I was pale and dark-haired, dark-eyed, and as I stood there it occurred to me suddenly that I looked like the boy I'd imagined Frankie to be in those days before I'd actually seen him. Only I was green as grass. Frankie wasn't.

'The thing is,' said John, and I could tell from his voice he'd decided I was too green to understand the thing he wasn't going to tell me, 'Etta's ambitious, like I said before. He wants to get to the top.'

'The top?' He was right, I didn't understand.

'In the Church. He wants to be a bishop one day. Or an archbishop, or even higher, who knows?'

'But what's that got to do with Frankie?'

'Frankie? He's that kid who came late, isn't he? The big blond kid from out west? The good-looking one?'

It startled me to hear him say this. Good-looking. Frankie was. I blushed. 'Yes.'

John caught at a strand of ivy and pulled off a leaf. He studied it for a moment before he looked up at me. 'Well, look, let's just say, Etta gets these *downs* on people. Then he thinks they're in his way—in the way of his getting on, I mean—so then he wants them out, see?'

'But why would he get a down on Frankie? How could Frankie get in his way?'

He sighed. 'Look, the best thing your Frankie can do is keep out of his way. Tell him to try and keep out of trouble, even small kinds of trouble, like being late. Etta's really good at making small things add up to something big. He writes stuff down. He's got this notebook he keeps in his pocket, I call it the Book of Little Things. He's probably got a few entries on your mate already, so tell him to be careful, eh?'

A bell rang. 'You'd better go,' he said. 'No sense in you being late too.'

As I began to hurry away he called after me, 'Take care.' Take care—it wasn't the common expression it is today and I remember it gave me a faint feeling of alarm, as if John Rushall thought I was in a dangerous place.

*

The class I had that period was Philosophy. Frankie's was Latin, which he hadn't done at his old school. His classroom was two doors up from mine, I'd pass it on my way. I still hadn't spoken to him that morning. He hadn't come up to me after breakfast and I wondered if he felt embarrassed about the private stuff he'd told me last night. I should have known better, even then. Frankie wasn't the kind of person who got anxious about such things. And I needn't have worried because when I passed the window of the Latin class Frankie looked up as I looked in, and his face lit up when he saw me and he waved.

His Latin teacher was Dr Gorman. Dr Gorman was tall and very thin, and the thick pebbly glasses he wore gave his narrow face a blind, foggy look. When he took them off you saw his eyes were sharp and clear. He was standing right in front of Frankie's desk. He looked at Frankie and then he looked out at me and back to Frankie again. Frankie hardly noticed him; he was still smiling and waving through the window. Dr Gorman took off his pebbly glasses and polished them with his handkerchief, then he put them on again, touched Frankie gently on the shoulder and said something to him. And then Frankie said something and Dr Gorman smiled and Frankie gave me one last wave and turned back to his notebook, and I felt suddenly so happy I could hardly breathe.

9.

'Tell him to try and keep out of trouble,' John Rushall had said, but this was impossible. Right from the start, Frankie was always in trouble. Most of it was small stuff: being late, running in the corridors, talking in class—Frankie loved to talk. Perhaps the girl down in Shoreham was only a little thing too, no more than a simple forgetting because he was new. Though I knew he still dreamed of her.

The real problem was that he stood out. We were not meant to stand out; we were supposed to forget our individual selves, submerge them in devotion to God. It wasn't that Frankie meant to draw attention to himself—he wasn't vain or conceited, he wasn't showing off—it was simply that there was something about him which drew people. He was like a warm light in a cold dark room. It was the brightness in him, I think, the way he delighted in the loveliness of the world, in all those ordinary things we were meant to put aside.

One breezy morning a group of us were crossing the courtyard on our way to chapel when Frankie stopped and pointed up towards the tower. It was a feast day, and the saint's flag was flying, flapping gaily with a clean snapping sound. 'I *love* that sound!' he said, turning to the rest of us, his eyes shining.

It was an odd thing to say, at least it was amongst a group of 1950s teenage boys, yet not one us tapped at his forehead or twirled a finger at his temple, or told Frankie he was barmy, like we might have done if it had been anyone else. I remember that morning so clearly: the blue sky, the little white clouds, the utter clarity of the air, in which the leaves of the bushes seemed to tremble with light—and the four of us, Frankie and me, Tim Vesey and Joey Gertler, all looking up at the banner and all of us listening intently to the sound of its flapping, in a way we never had before. We hadn't noticed, and now we did. We'd have missed so many things if it hadn't been for him. He *showed* us stuff, he really did. Everyone was smiling, and Tim said, 'Yeah, I love it too!'

On that glorious morning I was the only one who felt anxious. I was often like this when I was with Frankie. I was so happy to be with him that my whole body felt a kind of lightness, yet behind this airy happiness there was foreboding, a dark apprehension that at any moment this joy might be snatched away. I couldn't get John Rushall's words about Etta out of my head: 'He gets these *downs* on people—and then he wants them out.' Whenever Frankie and I were together, I'd be looking all round for Etta, in the shadows of a room or courtyard, in the trees at the edge of the playing field, up at a high window where a face might be. I'd listen for his footsteps in the corridor at night and I'd imagine him in his room, his big domed head bent over his notebook, writing down the little things that could add up to the big one for which Frankie could be sent away.

Frankie began sharing his food with the little kids, the ones who'd come to St Finbar's straight from primary school and slept in the long dormitory upstairs. At mealtimes he'd slip stuff into the big pockets of his cassock: a couple of sausages, a few slices of corned beef, roast potatoes, the iced buns we sometimes had for dessert, anything portable. It was hardly hygienic, but the little kids didn't care about the odd piece of fluff or a few grains of sand. When our meal was over, Frankie would share the stuff out in the small yard at the back of the refectory kitchen.

I was on the kitchen duty roster the day that he was caught and I saw the whole thing through the open kitchen window. We rarely had fruit at our meals, but that morning a fresh orange had miraculously appeared beside each plate, and there was Frankie outside in that dank little yard, surrounded by a crowd of the little kids, dividing oranges into segments for them. They were scrawny, these little kids, scrawny and scraggy, and they reminded me of the kids I'd seen at the old army camp playing in that muddy paddock like little ghosts in the dark. Close up you saw a kind of wildness in their eyes, as if they didn't know quite where they were, or how they'd got there, or why—and some of the St Finbar's kids had that look:

it seemed almost odd to see them laughing as they clustered round Frankie.

That kitchen yard was gloomy as the inside of a box, shadowed by walls on three sides, high windows glinting down. A tall hedge of prickly holly bounded the fourth side, a rough gateway cut into its centre. In my memory the scene has a kind of glow to it—the dark yard, the tall boy with the smaller ones gathered round him, all in their long black robes, so that the only colours were the pale gleam of blond hair and the vivid shocking dazzle of the oranges. It was like leafing through some dry old book and coming unexpectedly on a beautiful picture shut inside the dusty pages.

He had six oranges. Six! Standing there at the window I remember feeling a tiny stab of jealousy wondering which kids at his table had given their fruit to him. I envied them. I didn't like this envy or the growing desire I felt to have Frankie all to myself, yet I could do nothing about it. Such feelings seemed to have become a part of me. They had taken hold.

There was no one else in the kitchen, the other kids on duty roster had already gone, and the nuns who did the domestic work at St Finbar's didn't arrive till ten. I glanced up at the high windows of the building on the far side of the courtyard, they caught the sun and glared back at me. You couldn't see if there was anyone behind the glass, and I thought of Etta looking down, the Book of Little Things in his hand. There was nothing in our rule book that said you couldn't keep your food back and share it with the others, but I knew this was only because the rule makers hadn't thought of it; they hadn't imagined a situation where a kid might give his food away. If they had, there'd have been a rule for sure. Everything was like that in St Finbar's; behind the printed rules there were others you only found out when you broke them, though you always had a shadowy sense that they were there.

I pushed the window open. I was about to call out to Frankie when heavy footsteps sounded on the path beyond the hedge. The little kids went quiet. I saw one of them shove his orange pieces into his pocket and put his hands behind his back quickly, the others simply waited to see if the person out there would come through the gate or pass by harmlessly. Frankie went on peeling another orange, quite unconcerned, like a person from another world. The footsteps came nearer. If I'd thought about it for a moment I'd have worked out from the heaviness of those steps that it couldn't be Etta; Etta was too light, his feet too small to make that solid sound. It was Father Stuckey who walked in through the gate in the hedge.

He was the youngest of our teachers, a big shy man with spiky brown hair and a plain eager face with bright red cheeks like a child's. He taught the junior classes their ordinary school subjects and took all of us for sport. He loved sport, any kind, football and cricket and handball and tennis. We didn't have any tennis courts at St Finbar's but there was an old practice wall out near the vegetable gardens and sometimes you'd see Father Stuckey there with an old racquet, whacking a ball against the concrete for half an hour.

'Whoa!' he called as the little kids scattered past him like a flock of tatty black birds and disappeared through the hedge. He stared after them, shaking his head, and then turned back to Frankie, who stood there with a couple of oranges still in his hands. You could see Father Stuckey working it out, looking at the oranges and then back at the gap in the hedge where the kids had disappeared; putting two and two together and making a St Finbar's four. As I said, there was no written rule against keeping your food back and then giving it to others and Father Stuckey was no hardliner—all the same, when he began talking to Frankie you could see he was telling him not to do it again. I was pulling the window down when I heard Frankie cry out, 'But they're hungry!' And when he said this I saw Father Stuckey's whole body flinch and his big plain face flood with an expression you could only call shame. He put an arm round Frankie's shoulders and together they walked across the yard and out through the gate in the hedge.

*

It was true we were hungry sometimes, especially the youngest ones. By hungry I don't mean we were starved—we had three meals a day. We had meat: watery mince and corned beef and sausages and roast lamb on Sundays; we had boiled vegetables: potato and carrots and pumpkin; we had desserts: rice pudding or iced buns or steamed pudding with bright yellow custard. And bread, lots of it, as much as we could eat, though only one slice with butter. So we had food; it was simply that it never seemed enough. There was a raw feeling in our stomachs most of the time. Joey Gertler in my Philosophy class told me he thought about food all day and when he woke at night he'd picture the ingredients of the special hamburgers you could buy at the fish-and-chip shop in his home town: soft brown fried onions, juicy red tomatoes, fried egg, fresh crisp lettuce, and then the meat itself: the deep rich colour of it, the melted fat in glistening runnels in the patty's ridges and grooves. 'I never knew food could make you cry,' he said.

If she'd heard all this my mother would have commented, 'It simply wasn't enough for growing boys.' And I could picture my father frowning slightly, compressing his lips as if he'd expected exactly this kind of thing. I thought about my parents often; I thought about how they hadn't wanted me to come and how, in my eagerness, I'd felt they didn't understand. Sometimes angry tears would rush into my eyes. It was anger for myself, not them.

I'd had letters from them both. My mother wrote about my friends from school and the people in the neighbourhood. 'We all miss you,' she said. My father told me there'd been another epidemic of whooping cough amongst the children in the old army camp. 'We kept them all, this time,' he said, and he added at the bottom, 'Remember we are always here.'

I found it hard to answer these letters. We wrote home on Thursdays, and I would sit there for most of the hour, my mind frozen, trying to think what to write. In the relatively short time since I'd left home—two months it was, though it felt like years—I'd changed. The longing for glory had faded, and I'd lost that feeling of closeness to God. This was normal for the early days, my spiritual advisor told me. He was an elderly man called Father Barlow, who came up once a month from a theological college in the city. I was shedding false romanticism, he told me. Later on, as I became more robust in my faith, my sense of God would return. I must have patience, most of all I must have faith. I should concentrate on prayer. His very words, the utterly familiar words 'faith' and 'prayer' filled me with a wild impatience; I felt an urge to cry. They were like stones put in my mouth. Did Father Barlow notice? If he did he said nothing. Kneeling down beside him I would tense all over, fighting back the tears. How can you pray if the Being you're talking to seems to have gone away? It felt like talking to yourself. 'First sign of madness', people say, and sometimes I thought we were mad, all of us, stuck on that cold hillside, thinking we were the children of God. I didn't want to tell these things to my parents; I didn't want to tell them to anyone.

We wrote our letters in the library. I would glance across to the table where Frankie sat, his blond head bent over his letter, the left arm curved protectively around the sheet. I wondered if he was writing to that father who'd told him he'd offended Heaven, or the mother who'd whispered that she was too ashamed to say her prayers; I wondered if he got letters back. If he did he never said anything about them.

I couldn't tell my parents about Frankie, not properly. I

told them I'd made friends with the boy in the room next to mine, and how he'd come from this little town out west, but I couldn't describe him to them. I couldn't tell them about the deep indigo colour of his eyes and how it made me feel rich, or about the buttery gold of his hair, the satiny texture which made me want to touch it—these details were secrets, precious and somehow dangerous. I couldn't tell them how important he was to me, how he was becoming the best thing in my world. I couldn't tell anyone, I hardly admitted it to myself. And I said nothing about Etta. In the last minutes before the bell I'd panic, longing to share with them like I used to do, only I couldn't, I couldn't—I'd scribble a few pathetic lines about what we were studying in classes and what sports we played. I knew it wasn't enough. I knew it didn't even sound like me. I knew they'd notice, yet there was no way I could think how to put it right. I couldn't sound as I used to sound. Something was happening to me.

'Of course it was,' said Miri when I told her all this. 'You were starting to grow up. And beginning to fall in—'

'Don't!' I hushed her. 'Don't say it, Miri.'

You can never hush Miri. She picked up the edges of her sensible tweed skirt like a little girl at a dancing school recital. *Plonk!* went her stout brogues on the wooden boards of my veranda. *Plonk! Plonk!* Then she stood still, clasping her hands at her waist like a little girl about to recite a poem, and began to sing softly,

Falling in love again
Never wanted to
What am I to do
'Stop it, Miri!'

Of course she didn't stop. Nothing ever stopped Miri.

I can't help it!

'No more!' But I was laughing, and though it must have been at least thirty years then from my time at St Finbar's and I was getting on for fifty, I swear my face grew warm and I was blushing like some sad old lovelorn teenager.

10.

Hayden Jarrell was the smallest of the young kids in the dormitory upstairs. With his narrow pointed face and skinny limbs he looked barely older than nine. 'Hay', his friends called him ('Hey, hey, Hay!') and it suited his straw-coloured hair and the sandy skin speckled all over with freckles the size of threepenny bits.

'He comes from up my way,' Frankie told me one afternoon when a group of us were out clearing scrub to extend the vegetable gardens. 'Way out past Yulla it is—this little place right on the edge of the desert; blink when you're passing through and you'd miss it for sure.' He threw down his pick and cupped his hands together and it was like he was holding Hay Jarrell's little town between his palms. He made you see it: the wide main street with its dusty peppercorns, the general store that was also the bank and the post office, the single petrol pump outside, a couple of parked utes and a dog stretched out in a skinny piece of shade. 'He misses it,' said Frankie. 'And his family. He's an only, like you—so there's just him and his mum and dad. Imagine.' He shook his head and grabbed up the pick and took a swing at the stony ground. 'I bet they really love him.'

I forgot. I didn't think of the things he'd told me about his family: the beatings, the silences, the absence of love. 'Of course they love him,' I said. 'They're his mum and dad, aren't they?' Even as I spoke the words too fast, too fast, I sensed the hurt there might be in them for him and I could have bitten out my tongue. He said nothing and the look he gave me I couldn't work out, not then, anyway. It was neither scornful nor reproachful, it was the kind of look you might give a little kid who couldn't help saying stupid things because he was too young to know anything.

'Hay's only eleven,' he went on. 'Can you imagine being eleven and being here? Can you remember eleven?'

I thought of certain lovely days. 'Yeah,' I said. 'Yeah, I can.'

We went back to chopping at the stony soil in silence. When we paused for breath he said, 'He's got this little stammer. Have you noticed?'

'Hay?'

'Yeah. He says he didn't have it before. He says this place frightens him, and some of the people—well, he's only little. I told him it's no good being scared of people; if you get scared, then they win.'

'Yeah.' I thought of Etta, of course. I still had the feeling that if I said his name to Frankie it would be like pressing a button on some dreadful mechanism. It was now almost two months since that afternoon down in Shoreham and nothing had ever come of it—that didn't mean it wasn't written down in Etta's Book of Little Things, of course, yet though I watched for him all the time, I'd never once actually seen him spying on Frankie. There'd been no repetition of that strange stare I'd witnessed down in Shoreham which, when I recalled it, could still send a shiver down my spine. Just because I didn't see him watching didn't mean he wasn't there.

'Some people are scary,' I said uneasily.

Frankie stuck his pick in the ground and leaned on it. 'Like who?' His indigo eyes stared straight into mine. Still I said nothing.

'Like who?' he repeated.

'Well, the Rector,' I said, at last. 'He'd scare the little kids.'

Rufus Bowles was Rector at St Finbar's. Red, the senior boys called him, and the name had nothing to do with his politics; it was given for the fits of rage which shook him from time to time, when his deep voice roared out and the great vein above his left eye twisted and writhed as if it would burst right through the skin. These days they'd say he had an anger management problem and send him off to do a course, though I doubt any course could have coped with Red. It was like he *needed* to be angry, like he was hungry for it, always looking for some titbit to make him mad. He roamed the grounds and cloisters and though his black button eyes were cast down on the pages of his breviary, we knew he was really spying on us. At mealtimes those small eyes scoured the tables for any misdemeanour: a laugh, a sneeze, the clatter of a dropped piece of cutlery could bring forth a roar which seemed to shake the very walls, and the little kids trembled, we all trembled, even big Father Stuckey up at the high table, watching Red's huge meaty fingers tear at the soft insides of a bread roll.

He didn't scare me in the same way Etta did. He was in a different category, an angry man, that was all. Etta was something you couldn't define and I thought this might even be what made him scary. 'Yeah, the Rector,' murmured Frankie, smiling a little. 'Old Red. Yeah, Hay's scared of him all right.'

*

A couple of days later, Father Gorman came up to Frankie as we were coming out from breakfast. He had a message he wanted delivered to the bookbinder's hut. The hut was out on the other side of the dairy, at least half a mile away. 'You might be a bit late for class,' he said, 'so I'm giving you one of these,' and he handed Frankie one of the pink slips we called pinkos, that were used for late excuse. 'Don't lose it, eh?'

I kept an eye out for him through the window of my classroom. It looked out onto the courtyard and the cloister, the way Frankie would return. Half an hour into the lesson there was no sign of him. A small boy appeared at the far side of the courtyard, hurrying across it towards the door we used to go up to our rooms. It was Hay Jarrell, and even from a distance you could see that he had a streaming cold. His small face was flushed and his nose was running; he had a drowned look, parched for air, yet sodden. He reached up to the handle of the door, all the time glancing furtively around him because there was a rule that after breakfast you weren't allowed to go back to your room or dormitory—we weren't allowed back all day. It was supposed to teach you foresight, I think, forward planning of your day. It was obvious that Hay had forgotten to bring his hanky; he gave a sneeze so enormous that it bent his small frame double. When he straightened he shook himself like a puppy and wiped his nose on the sleeve of his cassock. Then he reached for the door again, and at that very moment the Rector's burly figure hurtled from the office on the other side of the courtyard.

It was clear that something had already made him angry that morning—he was bristling with it, dark in the face, his coarse black hair stiff with electricity. When he spotted Hay by the door he snorted, and his massive chest seemed to swell against the cloth of his soutane. 'Boy!'

Hay froze as the Rector charged towards him.

'Boy! What are you doing there?'

'I—I—'

'Were you about to go through that door?' Red took a step closer and jabbed a finger at Hay's narrow chest. 'Were you?'

Hay shrank back, so the finger was left jabbing at the air. 'Y-yes, Father.'

'Don't you know the rule? No one, I repeat, *no one* is allowed into the rooms or dorm during the day!'

'But, but I needed to get a hanky—'

The Rector reached his great hand towards him, and for a second I thought he was going to pick Hay up by the collar and give him a good shaking. I think we all thought that, because by this time the whole class was watching, even Father Beasely, who'd turned round from the board. Old Blinky, we called him, because he had a sleepy look and once or twice he'd dozed off at his desk, his big head propped on his hand. Now he was wide awake, staring through the window at Hay and the Rector, the chalk trembling in his hand. The window was open, we could hear every word, and a relieved sigh went round us when after all Red's hand descended harmlessly to his side. 'No one,' he roared again, '*no one* is allowed inside the building *during the day*. This is something you should have learned. Repeat it.'

Hay goggled up at him. 'What?'

'Repeat the *rule*.'

'Um. Um, no one is a-allowed, to—um,' he paused and then finished in a rush, 'to go inside during the day.'

'Remember it in future.'

'But I've got a c-cold,' said Hay doggedly. 'I need my hanky.'

We watched, amazed. Hay was so small he barely came up to the Rector's waist. He was like a little holly bush in the shadow of a gigantic oak. Although it was too far away to make out, we all knew the vein would be bulging in the Rector's temple.

'Please can I go and get my hanky, then?'

In the ordinary world, at this point, someone would have

yelled out, 'For God's sake, let the kid go and get his bloody hanky!' At St Finbar's, we acted differently. No one said a word, except for Old Blinky, who shook his head sorrowfully and murmured, 'Oh, Rufus!' so softly you could barely hear.

'Can I?' pleaded Hay again. His straw-coloured hair stood up stiffly in the breeze.

'No, you can't,' snapped the Rector, and abruptly, as if he'd had enough and any further sight of the small sniffling kid was more than he could bear, he turned sharply and stalked away. Hay stood staring after him, bewildered, as if he simply couldn't comprehend a world where your nose is running and you're sneezing and you're not allowed to go and get your handkerchief.

A breeze sprang up. Bold shadows danced along the walls. Frankie came running out of the cloister. He saw Hay and went straight up to him; a sudden wind whipped their words away but you could guess what they were saying. We could see Frankie searching in his pockets for a hanky, finding nothing, and then unbuttoning the top of his cassock and pulling out the bottom half of his shirt, grasping the cloth in both hands and tearing off a big square piece of it. And though we couldn't hear that either we could imagine the sound of it, sudden and shocking and somehow *clean. Riii—iip!* Like the sound of the flag on the tower snapping in the wind. Hay's face lit up, first with astonishment and then with glee. He laughed, and Frankie laughed with him, and a moment later Hay was running down the steps to his class, clutching the makeshift hanky. Frankie sauntered off to his own class, hands in his pockets, slowly, untroubled. I think he might even have been whistling. Old Blinky turned back to his notes on the board and we went back to our copying.

What is it that makes you sense another person is staring at you? Back at my primary school, old Sister Honoria would have said it was your guardian angel. I wasn't sure that I believed in guardian angels anymore—all I can say is that I felt the gaze upon my skin. It was like cold oil. I looked up and out of the window again and Etta was in the courtyard. He stood exactly in its centre, and his dark sharp shadow stretched out from him like the marker on a sundial. Those strange deep-set eyes were fixed on me, and the gaze was quite different from the one he'd fixed on Frankie down in Shoreham, in which, without actually registering it at the time, I'd sensed a kind of longing. There was no longing in the way he looked at me across the courtyard, simply a chilling and intense dislike, which at first I didn't recognise. Then I did. It was more than dislike, it was hate—for some reason I couldn't fathom, Etta hated me and he wanted me to know. I was shocked. I had lived a very sheltered life; no one had hated me before. I tried to think of reasons: did he hate me because he knew I tried to keep Frankie out of those troubles Etta needed for his Book of Little Things? It never occurred to me for a moment that the hatred might spring from jealousy.

'Mr Rowland, are you with us today?'

I looked round to find Old Blinky standing beside my desk.

'Ah, you are with us. Then if you could kindly translate for us the first two paragraphs of chapter three?'

I translated. When I finished, and looked through the window again, Etta was gone. He had such an ease in appearing and disappearing that you wondered if you'd really seen him at all. He was like smoke. Sometimes I thought I smelled a whiff of sulphur in the air.

11.

As the weeks passed and there was nothing to remind him and no chance of seeing her, I'd thought Frankie would gradually forget the girl from St Brigid's. But he didn't forget. If anything, his preoccupation with her seemed to grow more intense. Almost every night he talked to me about her; he had the most exact memory of that encounter, those few precious moments on the road below the seminary. Every detail seemed to have imprinted itself on his imagination: her hair, her lips, her eyes. To talk about her skin—its softness, the flush of colour on her cheekbones—could make him breathless. It was the greatest disappointment to him that he hadn't heard her voice, that she hadn't spoken, only smiled. 'Though if I had to choose,' he said, 'I'd rather have the smile. Did you see it, Tom? I think she liked me. Do you think she liked me or do you think she was just being kind because she felt sorry for me?'

'Sorry for you? Why would she feel sorry for you?'

'Oh, you know. All dressed up in my black crow's outfit. All dressed up and nowhere to go.'

'She liked you.'

'You think so?'

'Yes.'

I could sense his pleasure, even through the wall. 'What do you think her name is? I bet it's beautiful too—' And he started going through a list of girls' names, all the ones he liked most: Teresa and Barbara and Rosalind and Clare...

He dreamed of her continually. Lying awake, which had become a habit with me, first out of homesickness then from my anxiety about Etta, I'd become familiar with Frankie's dreams and I could tell when they were about her. Those dreams were full of shifting restlessness and a kind of deep yearning I swear I could feel right through the wall. I knew he was dreaming of making love with her like he'd done with Manda Sutton. Then one night he had the nightmare again, the one he'd had a few days after he'd first arrived. 'No!' he was shouting, 'no, Dad, no!' It was worse this time—he was crying in big gasping sobs like the kids with whooping cough brought into my father's surgery, where it seemed with each gasp that they'd never be able to catch their breath again. I went to him. I jumped out of bed and ran out from my room into his without a thought that I was breaking rules. I pushed his door open and the moon gleamed down from that high strip of window like the face of a wicked old man. Frankie was sitting up in bed with his hands clenched on the blanket. I could feel the terror coming off him like heat. 'It's all right, it's all right,' I whispered, and he stared at me blankly, still half asleep, half in the nightmare.

I switched on the light.

'I didn't! I didn't!' he shouted.

'It's me, it's me, it's Tom.' I grasped one of his hands. It was warm and rough, and the suddenness of that contact gave me a kind of shock. I felt as if, in my whole life, I'd never really touched anyone before. I sat down on the bed, still with his hand in mine. He was waking properly now—I could see it in his eyes, like a tide coming in, see him starting to work out where he was and who I was and what I was doing there.

'Tom?'

'You were having a nightmare,' I explained. 'It sounded bad, so—so I came in.'

He leaned back against the pillow, though he kept his hand in mine. 'It was my dad,' he said.

'Your dad?'

'I was dreaming about him. He was angry.' A little shudder ran through him, I felt it in the bones of his hand.

'It was only a dream.'

He bit at his bottom lip. He had big square teeth, very white and strong-looking. 'I know, but he did get angry, Dad. He got angry a lot.' His face took on that same baffled, stricken expression I'd noticed the time we were coming through the cloisters and he'd told me how his dad used to make them sit quiet when they got home from church while he said the whole mass again.

'He loves us, but,' he said. He must have seen my uncertainty, right there, because he added, 'Honest he does! It's just he gets

– 92 –

fed up sometimes. With work, you know, and having so many mouths to feed. And with me being no good. Scum.'

The word shocked me. I couldn't even say it. 'You're not!'

'Thanks.' He smiled and his hand slipped out of mine as he settled his head down onto the pillow. There was a button hanging loose on his pyjama top and I couldn't take my eyes off it: I wanted to snatch it, to keep. It was the most ordinary sort of button, plain white, with four tiny holes where the cotton went through. I couldn't understand why I wanted it so much. He closed his eyes and I got up from the bed and went towards the door. When I was halfway there he called out, 'Tom!'

I turned. 'Yeah?'

He was sitting up again. 'Manda Sutton and me, what we did, you know, what I told you about that time, when Dad caught us...I've been thinking and thinking, and it wasn't bad, not like everyone makes out. Really it wasn't.' He was looking at me almost beseechingly, and somehow I knew that he wasn't only talking about Manda Sutton, but about the girl down in Shoreham, those dreams he had of her.

'It was lovely,' he said. 'With Manda. Truly it was. Do you believe me?'

I thought of the beautiful dusk falling and Frankie singing in it, and the little green stars and the cherry trees, and I tried not to think of Manda Sutton and especially not the dark-haired girl because I knew he was thinking of doing the same thing with her, and thinking how lovely that would be. I said, 'Yes, I believe you.'

'Say it then.'

'What?'

'Say it was lovely.'

'It was lovely.' I switched off the light and his voice came to me through the dark. 'So how can something that's so lovely be bad? How come it's supposed to be this great big sin?'

'I don't know,' I said. 'I don't know, Frankie.'

Outside in the corridor there was a perfect quiet. It was a still moony night and there wasn't a sound from the small kids upstairs and I hoped they were asleep and hadn't heard any sound from Frankie's nightmare. I'd just reached my door when I heard a creak on the stairs. At once I thought of Etta. I froze, my hand on the doorknob, my fingers unable to turn it. He'd have seen the light in Frankie's room, he must have— or else he'd been prowling round the corridors and heard the sound of the nightmare and our doors opening and closing. My heart thudded—any second I expected to see that strange domed head rising up the stairs. I don't know how long I stood there, my gaze fixed on the spot where he would appear. No one came, and after what seemed like an hour but was probably no more than a few minutes, I crept down to the landing and peered over the banisters. The stairs were empty all the way down to the next floor and in the dim light of the single overhead lamp the polished wood of the next floor looked like a sheet of gold.

Back in my room I began to wonder if I'd imagined that creaking sound, if it was in my head, part of my fear that Etta would get Frankie thrown out and I'd never see him again. I lay on my bed and for the first time I thought about why the idea of losing Frankie frightened me so much, when I'd only known him such a little while. I told myself it was because I was lonely and missing my home, though that didn't really seem enough. Then I thought it was because Frankie was special and if I lost him I'd never find anyone so special again, for me. That seemed right.

Suddenly I remembered Denny and Joseph back home. There was this night when my father was called out to the army camp, and I'd gone with him. It was a bad night, drizzling and bitterly cold. 'You stay in the car,' he said. 'I won't be long.' He was long, though, so long that I went to find him. The cold iron huts had narrow corridors and small poky rooms where doors stood open on cot beds pushed together in a jumble of blankets and newspapers and clothes, little crowded kitchens dark as dens. A small girl leaning against a doorway kicked at me as I went past. 'What do *you* want?' Someone was crying somewhere.

My father was in the room with the crying. A woman lay on a bed and he was bandaging her arm. She had a black eye and there was a red mark on her shoulder the size of a big fist. A man slumped in a corner, neighbours stood peering round the door. 'Here's your boy, Doc,' one of them said, and my father glanced up for a second but he didn't say anything. He finished bandaging the woman's arm and said to her gently, 'I'd like you to come to the surgery tomorrow, Mrs Lightman.' She didn't answer and he said to one of the neighbours, 'Mrs

Carter, do you think you could come to the surgery with Mrs Lightman?' Mrs Carter nodded and my father smiled at them, and then we walked out of the place; and halfway across that muddy stinking field, he said to me, 'Don't ever let anyone tell you poverty is holy.' Then he strode on again, so fast I had to run to keep up with him.

The light rain was still falling as we drove away down Lascelles Avenue and into China Road. Denny and Joseph lived in China Road, in a small cottage with a huge old peppercorn tree in the middle of the front yard. Most of the houses in the street were dark already, but the window of Den and Joseph's living room was fairly ablaze with light, the curtains undrawn, and you could see them seated at the table playing a board game. Denny made a move and then Joseph made one and then Den clapped his hand over Joseph's and they both started laughing. You could feel their happiness, it seemed to fill the room and pour out through the windows towards us; all at once I felt warm and my father was smiling. 'See?' he said. 'It's the love that counts. Always.'

*

In my room at St Finbar's, I pulled the blanket close around me. Next door Frankie had fallen dreamlessly asleep. I could hear his breathing, soft and slow and even; it reminded me of the sound of the sea on still days, shusha, shusha, shusha. It lulled me—I don't know what I would have done if it hadn't been there.

12.

Frankie found a photograph in one of the big leather-bound collections of old St Finbar's magazines that were kept in the shelves at the back of the library. It showed a group of St Finbar's boys sitting on the grass in front of the old dairy. The dairy wasn't so old back then; though the photograph was in faded black-and-white you could see the boards were freshly painted, they had a kind of gleam. It must have been a special day because at one side of the photograph you could see the end of a trestle table with a white cloth spread, and a big glass jug with glasses stacked beside it. Behind them in the distance the flag was flying from the tower.

In the list of names beneath the photograph there were two which were familiar: Rufus Bowles and Lionel Beasely, the Rector and Old Blinky. Lionel Beasely wore old-fashioned wire-rimmed glasses and a jaunty smile; it was a kind face, and it was easy to imagine Old Blinky being that sort of child. Rufus Bowles was the big surprise: the Rector was as small and skinny as Hay Jarrell. Without the pouches of flesh his black button eyes were larger, softer—he looked like the kind of kid who might write poetry at night. 'See his hand,' said Frankie, and I looked and saw how the thin kid was holding his hand out to the camera and there was a small white butterfly perched on the back of it.

'You wouldn't believe,' said Frankie.

He borrowed more of the old journals from the library and pored over the photographs. At night I heard the pages turning as he searched for names we knew: he found Father Nolan from his own town and Father Max, the principal of my old school. He found Father James: a long-faced, dreamy boy.

He caught up with me on the stairs one night after evening prayers. I knew his footsteps by then, the special sound of them; I knew his light touch on my arm. 'Look!' he exclaimed. He was carrying another journal beneath his arm. We stood on the landing beside Tim Vesey's window. It was dark and the headland was dotted with lights, and I thought how Tim knew which light was home. Frankie rested the book on the window ledge and turned the pages. He'd found Father Gorman. Young Patrick Gorman was holding a cup won by the senior debating team; he was beaming and his hair was mussed and the buttons of his cassock were done up crookedly, like Frankie's often were. 'See, he looks just like us!' He stared down at the picture for a long time and once he put a hand up to his face and felt the bones as if to test they were still solid. Kids hurried past us up the stairs, occasionally casting curious glances in our direction. 'Come on,' I said, 'we'd better go.'

After lights out that night he tapped on the wall and brought up the subject again—how they looked like us in those pictures. 'Did you see Father Gorman! And think of him now!'

'Everyone gets old,' I said.

'No, no, it's not that, it's not old, I mean. They've got a *look*. Father Stuckey's got it, and he's not old. Not *really* old. It's something else, it's—they get a look about them like they're not quite the real thing.'

I thought of Father James on those evenings he came to dinner at our place. You could see how he tried to fit in, to be like us, only he could never quite get it right. Even those sly adoring glances he gave my mother had a strangely made-up quality, as if he was holding his breath, thinking to himself, 'I'm doing *this, now.*'

There was a fabric around in those days called artsilk. My mother had a dress made from it, my favourite of all her dresses, pale blue forget-me-nots on a dark blue background. I thought it made her look beautiful; when she put it on her hair seemed darker, cloudier. My father liked it too. 'Oh, that old artsilk thing!' she'd say whenever we pestered her to wear it, and for a long time, with that blue dress in mind, I thought the word 'artsilk' meant the material was a kind of work of art, special and beautiful. Then one day she told me the word was simply a shortened way of saying artificial silk, and artsilk wasn't real silk, though it looked and felt like it. 'They're artsilk,' I said to Frankie. 'Our teachers. They look like real people, but they're really manufactured.'

I thought he'd laugh, I'd meant it jokingly—instead he said very seriously, 'I'm not going to let that happen to me, I'm not *ever* going to get that look.'

'I was only joking.'

'No, it's true. And you can start looking like that when you're young, too. Tom?'

'Yeah?'

'Do I still look okay?'

'Of course you do.'

'Because *she* wouldn't like it. She wouldn't like going around with a boy who looked like he wasn't the real thing.'

He had begun to talk like this recently—as if he really knew the girl down in Shoreham, as if they were going out together. Though I knew it was only a sort of game—the habit of mind you might get from thinking about a person continually, so that they became a kind of imaginary companion in your private world—it was disturbing. I think we all played games: Tim Vesey at his window, watching the lights of his house go out, whispering goodnight to the people up there, pretending they could hear. Or the way, crossing the paddock to the football field, I would sometimes stand still on the springy grass, imagining I was standing on that old brown doormat back home, screwing my eyes shut tight, playing the game that when I opened them I'd actually be there. Frankie imagining he had a beautiful girlfriend down in the town. At the heart of all these games was love: for Tim and me it was the love we'd known at home, Frankie looked for his love elsewhere.

*

Mirrors were in short supply at St Finbar's. There were a few small ones in the bathroom for the boys who shaved, though if you were as tall as Frankie it was difficult to see the upper half of your face. And the glass was spotted with mildew, so your skin had a leprous look. He took to seeking his reflection in the dark windows of the refectory, and in puddles of rain, even in the shiny distorting hollow of his porridge spoon. One evening after night prayers I found him in the broad corridor below our stairway. It was lined with portraits of former rectors and church dignitaries. He was standing before a full-size portrait of the Archbishop, whose dark robes framed behind the glass formed a perfect mirror.

'Look! I can see myself!' he said delightedly. 'The *whole* of myself! And I'm still all right.'

'I told you.'

Behind his glass the Archbishop gazed out at him sternly. Frankie leaned up close and stretched his arms along the portly image. 'Look! I'm hugging the Archbishop, see!' He stood on tiptoe and planted a kiss on the dim painted lips. 'Mwaa! Look! I'm kissing him now!'

The corridor where we stood gave onto a narrower passageway, and from there I now heard footsteps approaching. Soft ones. 'Someone's coming,' I whispered. Frankie wasn't bothered. Steps behind him, the idea of some unseen person watching—these things never seemed to trouble him, he trusted people. He was unwary, and I wished with all my heart that I could have been like that. But I wasn't, I knew it, and standing there in the corridor I vowed I would look out for him so he never became anxious and fearful like me.

'Mwaa!' He stepped back from the portrait and blew the Archbishop another kiss just as the unseen person emerged from the passageway. It was Father James. He was wearing his black clerical overcoat and his shoes gleamed and he looked happy. A set of car keys dangled from his hand—he was going out, and I thought with a pang how this might be one of those times when he visited my parents, one of those nights when he arrived very late, and he and my father sat talking till morning.

'Hello Frankie, hello Tom,' he said. 'On your way upstairs?'

'Just going,' said Frankie cheerfully. 'We're saying goodnight to the Archbishop.'

Father James laughed. The laugh died abruptly and he was frowning past us to the pool of shadows at the bottom of the stairs. I looked round. Etta was standing there. All the time he'd been standing there, all the time when Frankie had been peering at his reflection and kissing the painted Archbishop behind his glass—acts which would fill a whole page of Etta's Book of Little Things.

'Brian Cooley,' said Father James softly. For a moment the name didn't register, even though John Rushall had told me that it was Etta's real one. Frankie had never heard of it. 'Brian Cooley?' he said, and then he laughed delightedly, 'Brian Cooley. He's Brian Cooley!'

The reiteration of his true name had a strange effect on Etta. I can't describe it except to say that some movement on his face reminded me of a sudden ripple on a still dark pool: something's there beneath the water, only nothing breaks the surface, nothing comes. I sensed a hidden fury and thought of the story, *Rumpelstiltskin,* where the manikin was so angry when the miller's daughter called out his true name that he tore himself in two.

'Father James?' Etta stepped out of the shadows.

'Brian?'

Etta pointed at Frankie. 'This boy—'

'Frankie,' said Father James.

'Francis Maguire,' said Etta, and there was a hint of wetness in his voice as he spoke Frankie's name. 'Francis Maguire was being disrespectful.'

'Disrespectful?'

'He was making fun of the Archbishop's portrait.'

'Was he now?'

'He—kissed it.'

'Kissed it!' said Father James. 'Well, that must have been a surprise for His Eminence.' He swayed a little and it struck me suddenly that he might be drunk. Only a little bit though.

'And he was looking at himself.'

'What?'

'He was looking at his reflection in the glass, Father. *Admiring* himself.' Etta rose a little on his toes, then went down on his heels again, as if to emphasise the seriousness of the crime. 'That's vanity, Father. That's self love.'

'I don't love myself!' protested Frankie. 'I don't, do I, Tom?'

I said quickly, 'No, you don't,' and Father James looked from one of us to the other.

Etta ignored us. He concentrated his attention on Father James. 'Aquinas says self love is the cause of every sin.'

Thomas Aquinas was the theologian we studied most intensively at St Finbar's. He was called 'The Angelic Doctor'. There was a portrait of him hanging in the library; his round chubby face had an absorbed, dreamy expression—Frankie said he didn't look like the real thing.

'Aquinas, Brian?' said Father James. 'And didn't Aquinas say, after he saw that vision a little while before he died, that everything he'd written was straw in the wind compared to what he'd seen?'

Etta's face went blank. It was smooth though. Hiding things.

'Did he really have a vision, Father?' asked Frankie eagerly. He loved hearing about visions and miracles.

Father James nodded.

'What did he see?'

'No one knows exactly.'

'He saw Heaven,' exclaimed Frankie, and he stretched out his arms to all of us. 'I bet he saw Heaven!'

Frankie's religion was different from mine. He believed in Heaven quite literally, as if it was another lovely world out past the stars. He believed in angels and resurrected saints in golden robes and haloes: he pictured them walking with Jesus and Mary in fields where the lion lay down with the lamb. He believed they saw everything we did, heard every word we spoke, knew every thought in our minds. These glorious beings were the people he thought he'd offended by making love to Manda Sutton, the ones to whom he whispered, 'Sorry, sorry, sorry,' in the night. Mystical Rose, Tower of David, Tower of Ivory, House of Gold—whenever I hear that litany, I think of Frankie, because that's how he believed, and it seemed strange when you thought of that hot little desert town he came from, the frightening family life he sometimes described to me.

He caught hold of the sleeve of Father James' clerical coat and gave it a tug. 'He did see Heaven, didn't he?'

Father James smiled at him. 'I think perhaps he did. Now off you go upstairs, both of you; the bell's about to ring.'

'But Father James,' protested Etta. 'Father, this boy—' he pointed, 'Francis Maguire—' Again I heard that slick wet sound.

'And you too, Brian,' said Father James coolly, as if Etta was no more important than Frankie and me, only another student he was sending off to bed. 'You too may go.'

He and Etta stared at each other. It was a long stare, a long silent moment which seemed to stretch on and on so you thought something extraordinary would happen at the end of it. Only it never did. With a sudden click of his heels Etta turned and walked away down the corridor. Frankie and I went up the stairs. At the top I looked back, Father James was still standing at the door; he might have been watching to make sure that Etta didn't return. He waved to us and pulled open the door. It was raining outside. 'Ah, rain,' he said, and splashed out through the puddles.

*

'What do you think St Thomas *saw*?' Frankie asked me that night. 'Do you think he saw Heaven?'

'I don't know.'

He was silent. I heard him shifting in his bed and imagined him lying there looking up at the ceiling, the soft buttery hair on the pillow, his hands clasped behind his head. 'I think that would be the best thing,' he said. 'To see Heaven.'

I didn't know what happened to me then—that sudden harsh surge of rage that swept through me so that I wanted to shout at him, 'Do you? Do you? The best thing? Better than fucking Manda Sutton? Better than fucking that girl from St Brigid's?'

Of course I said nothing like this. I was priggish about words like 'fuck' and I hated people shouting. I don't think I would have been able to shout at Frankie, anyway, I wouldn't have got past the first couple of words. But I wanted to. Why did I feel so angry? So violent? Was I jealous of those girls? Jealous of him wanting them, dreaming of them? Or was it something else? Was I, without knowing it, angry because I was beginning to feel that his childlike beliefs could pin him, still living, to a collector's board? At St Finbar's, things could build up inside you and you didn't know they were building. Even now I'm not sure what caused that anger, only that from this time on tides of anger and confusion would come rushing through my heart and then race out again, leaving me flat and sad.

'Tom?'

'Yeah?'

'Wouldn't it be the best thing? To see Heaven?'

Upstairs a small kid whimpered in the dormitory. The best thing, I thought savagely, would be if there wasn't any Heaven or any God and St Finbar's closed and that kid could go home to his mum and dad again. I didn't say any of that, either. I could hardly believe it was in my mind. 'Yes,' I said dully. 'Yes, it would be the best thing.'

13.

One afternoon at sport I couldn't find Frankie anywhere. I'd seen him across the refectory at lunchtime, afterwards I'd missed him in the crowd hurrying down towards the changing sheds. I wandered over to a group waiting for a turn at the handball court and asked if they'd seen him. No one had. They were talking about the holidays, what it would be like when the year ended and we'd be back home for two whole months, amongst ordinary people in the ordinary world. 'Funny,' said Joey Gertler. 'It's going to feel really funny.'

'Funny,' exclaimed Bri Tobin, and the word came out so roughly, almost savagely, that we all looked round. Bri was a big, strong boy who came from the same part of the city as I did, the sprawling suburbs over beyond the railway line. He reminded me of Jimmy Blewitt, the boy who'd come up to me at school the day Father Boyle had announced my vocation and said, 'Tom, it's forever.' Like he knew what 'forever' was.

'It's *this* place that's "funny",' Bri went on, still in that same savage voice. He jabbed a finger at the ground on which we stood. 'It's like they want us to think we're the only good ones. God's *Specials,* different from everyone else.'

'But we are different,' someone said. One person, I didn't see who it was. Everyone else was silent, listening, waiting to hear what else Bri was going to say. Normally he was a quiet boy; I think that's why we listened so intently, because now, as his voice speeded up, we sensed he couldn't stop talking even if he'd wanted to. 'You wake up in the middle of the night and you can't remember your little sister's name. How's that for being *different*, eh? How's that for being one of "God's Specials"? A couple of years more and if your mum went blind you wouldn't care because you wouldn't know how to care anymore. Not for *them*! Not for ordinary people!' His breath caught, he was almost sobbing, and I saw Joey Gertler put his hand up to his mouth as if to hold back some kind of answering sob. 'What would some ordinary lady going blind matter, anyway?' Bri went on. 'She's not important, she's an *extern*. She's not one of *us*.' He thumped a fist into his palm. 'I don't care what they say, thinking like that, it's wrong. It's bad. You feel like you're getting this little black hole inside you and it's getting bigger and bigger and some day you might even want to hurt people. And—and you won't even *know* you do.'

There were gasps. A couple of kids started talking in rushy voices about football teams, trying to drown him out, to pretend. Others inched away. I wished Frankie had been there. I went up to Bri. 'You're right.' I said.

But he didn't want to talk anymore. His face had gone

blotchy. 'No, sorry,' he blurted. 'Look, sorry, I shouldn't have said all that.' He turned and walked off towards the changing shed, his fist rubbing at his eyes.

Two years later, at the beginning of his senior year, Bri Tobin left St Finbar's. His place was vacant in the chapel and the refectory, and that was all we knew. Nothing was ever said officially, though the usual rumours sprang up: that his parents had thrown him out too, that he'd been seen up the Cross, drunk and chucking his guts out in the gutter. Someone had seen him begging with the old soldiers in the dark little arcade that ran between Wynyard and Hunter Street in those days. None of it was true. Bri went home and his parents were glad to have him there. He got a job in the post office and studied for his matriculation at night school; he went on to university and became a psychologist, married and had a family. The little black hole inside him closed over and he never became the kind of person who wanted to hurt people.

That afternoon after Bri strode off I looked around again for Frankie. There was still no sign of him and he should have been easy to spot: St Finbar's had no uniform for sport and most of us wore shorts and the sweaters from our old schools. They were sombre colours mostly—grey and navy and dark green—and Frankie's sweater stood out because it was bright red. All the same it was a while before I finally saw him, a flash of colour against the scrub, way up on the hillside near the wall where I'd walked with my parents that day back in summer. I hurried round the back of the handball courts and along the track that skirted the vegetable gardens. There was no one around to see me, or at least I didn't see anyone, though there were plenty of places to hide.

The wall had crumbled further since I'd last seen it. Stones lay in the grass and there was a big gap where you could stand and look down to the road without being seen from below. From there you could see straight over the walls into the garden of St Brigid's, its smooth green lawns like water in the bottom of a cup. It was mid-afternoon of a sunny day and the girls were out for their break, strolling in pairs along the gravel paths, scattered in little laughing groups beneath the big trees. I saw Frankie's girl at once. She had that same intense vitality Frankie had; your eyes were drawn to her. She was sitting on the grass with a friend and Frankie was watching her. He was taking in every detail: the way she laughed, throwing her head back to show her white throat, the way she was wearing her hair today, braided in one long thick plait and tied with a navy ribbon; and the way her face grew serious as she bent forward to listen to her friend, it made her seem so real. Frankie was like a thirsty person drinking from a glass; I saw his throat move as he swallowed. When she lifted a lock of the other girl's hair and wound it round her finger, I could see a kind of shiver move all the way down his spine.

'Frankie?'

He looked round. He didn't seem surprised to see me; perhaps he'd heard someone coming but that hadn't been enough to make him take his eyes from the girl. Now, for a moment, he did. 'Her name's Bella!' he said, and his eyes were shining.

I had never told him about Etta seeing him that day down in Shoreham; now without any warning, it came bursting out of me. It was those shining eyes, I think, and the way he'd said her name, with a kind of tender reverence, as if she was one of those holy creatures in his clear blue heaven. 'You'd better be careful,' I said, 'Etta's been watching you.'

He looked bewildered. 'Etta? You mean the prefect?'

'Yes.' I said the name again, tempting fate. 'Etta.' Nothing happened after all, no dreadful mechanism came grinding into life. A little breeze sprang up from nowhere, that was all, and Frankie shrugged and turned back to studying Bella down there in the garden. The navy ribbon was slipping down her braid and his eyes fastened on it. I could see he wanted that ribbon like I'd wanted the loose button on his pyjama shirt.

'He was watching you that afternoon down in Shoreham,' I went on. 'You know, when we were coming back from the dentist's, when you saw—Bella.'

He turned back to me. 'He was there?'

'Near that chemist's shop. He was watching you.' He didn't ask me why I hadn't told him before and I was glad, because out in the sunny afternoon the idea that if I said Etta's name to him it would be like pressing the button on some dreadful mechanism sounded barmy, though inside my head it still sounded right. 'John Rushall told me Etta gets these downs on people,' I went on. 'And then he tries to get them thrown out.'

'Thrown out? How?'

'He's got this notebook. He sort of collects all the times people get in trouble, even if it's little things like being late, and—'

'Or coming up here to look at girls,' he said, smiling. You could see he didn't really take it seriously. 'Or sneaking out at night.'

'You go out at night?' The minute he said it, certain things fell into place: those nights I'd wake and couldn't hear his breathing and there'd be a sense of emptiness from his room; the way I hardly ever saw him in the early mornings; and how, a couple of times, going down the stairs to morning prayers I'd met him coming up, already dressed, an air about him as if he'd been somewhere. I glanced down at the girl in the St Brigid's garden. Did he meet her? Were those happy dreams not dreams at all, but memories? My voice rushed, it ran. 'Do you go and meet her?'

He looked down at the girl and sighed. 'Oh, if I could. Only I can't—I promised, didn't I?'

'Promised?'

'In the church that time, back home. You know, before I came here. I made this—promise. So now, I just, well—mostly I just *walk*. I've got to—I wake up and I get so restless, I've got to go out and walk. There's lots of places—' He waved his arms. 'It's a lovely world. Sometimes I go to that place you told me about, that cliff above the sea, where you went with your mum and dad—'

'You go there?' I thought of the narrow pitted shelf, the murky little pools, my mother saying, *It's like a picture of the end.*

He grinned at me. 'Don't look like that. I like it there, it's great. When you sit on the ledge and look out, there's so much *space*, all that sea and sky, you can watch the sun come up—'

He'd get caught. That cliff top was out of bounds. I imagined Etta following him, creeping through that close green tunnel, only a little way behind.

He read my mind. 'Look, Etta won't see me. He's not *God*. Not even the devil. He's nothing—a kid who hates himself, that's all.'

'Hates himself?' Startled, I thought of Etta's immaculate appearance; the spotless cassock, the shining boots, the clean perfection of his tiny fingernails. 'How? How does he hate himself?'

Frankie shrugged. 'He just does. You can see it. There's lots of people like that—wrong. Wrong people, no matter how good they look from outside.' For a second, his face had that queer stricken expression it got when he spoke of his father.

A bell sounded from inside the convent and the girls began to drift towards the building. Bella and her friend got up from the grass and brushed down their skirts, then arm in arm they walked towards the door. The ribbon fell from Bella's plait and when he saw it Frankie drew in a breath, and I could see that the ribbon falling onto the grass and Bella stooping to pick it up were more important to him than anything I'd said about

Etta. The girls went inside and the garden was empty, yet we still stayed there beside the wall. I told him what Bri Tobin had said, and how people had walked away from him as if he had some disease that was catching, and he nodded and said, 'They're scared.'

Down on the road a man and woman came walking, their voices a low close murmur. The woman laughed suddenly, and the man smiled at her and caught her hand.

'They're so lucky,' sighed Frankie. 'To be in love, and it's just a happy, ordinary thing.' When he spoke the word 'love', you heard a kind of gravity in it, and at the same time an amazing lightness, so that the word seemed to spring free and fly into the air. You could almost see it, like a beautiful balloon you wanted to run after.

Down in the seminary, our own bell rang. It was the bell for study, and after that there'd be the bell for tea, and then rosary, and then more study, and fifteen minutes' walk around the courtyard, and then night prayers.

We set off down the hill.

14.

Winter came on. The wind howled, it flung itself against the walls, shrieking at the windows like a tribe of demons struggling to get in. The rain swept in great freezing sheets across the courtyard, icy puddles filled the hollows of the paving stones. The sea roared. One morning Frankie sneaked off to look at it from his secret perch on that narrow ledge above the sea. It was a little before dawn; in the grey light he would have seen the high swollen waves crash in, and the spray would have soared so high it drenched him through. He would have loved it. I met him coming up the stairs as the rest of us were hurrying down to chapel, and I went with him to his room and waited in the doorway while he brushed that sticky grey sand from his cassock and gathered up his books for classes. 'It was wonderful!' he told me. His face had a kind of raw happiness all over it, his hair stood in stiff salty spikes. 'I'm going to go there again!' I don't think he'd have felt the wind and rain, and if he did it would have been part of it all, another small glory of the lovely, lovely world. Standing there listening to him, it struck me that Etta, though he'd have no time for the loveliness of the world, would share this kind of invulnerability—bent on his own purposes, he'd hardly notice wet and cold. And again I imagined him creeping after Frankie along that grey sandy path through the blackberries and lantana—oblivious, intent.

I still couldn't properly understand that intent. Etta's ambition was clear enough to me, but I couldn't understand why Frankie should be in his way. I didn't see why he should 'get a down' on Frankie, as John Rushall had warned. 'He hates himself,' Frankie had said, and I didn't understand this either. Not then, anyway.

Oh, it was cold that winter! The stuff of our cassocks, so heavy and sweaty in those first weeks at the drag end of summer, now seemed thin as paper, the wind cut straight through. We had chilblains and cold sores, and coughing filled the classrooms and the chapel and the rooms and dormitories at night. A boy fainted in choir practice and was borne away by two prefects without the slightest break in our singing, the beautiful harmonies of Palestrina's *O Domine Jesu Christie* rising uninterrupted to the great rafters, and I felt we were no more than simple instruments of skin and flesh and bone.

The weather brought a fresh wave of homesickness to the small boys upstairs. As the weeks stretched to months they'd settled down as routines took over and their homes seemed further and further away. Now and again you'd hear a whimper in the middle of the night when one of them woke from a bad dream or a bad memory of the day, but most of them appeared to sleep soundly. Now winter made them cry again. I suppose the new weather brought fresh memories of home: rain running down the windows of a familiar room, wet umbrellas dripping in the hall, mothers in dressing gowns filling hot water bottles from kettles on stoves. I'd learned myself how memories could make you ache all over, make you feel like shouting, 'I want to *be* there!'

The sound of those small boys crying was terrible. I think it was the way they choked it off—how they knew they weren't supposed to cry, especially at night, in the middle of the Great Silence, because they were special people; they belonged to God, they should not long for earthly comforts, for their earthly mums and dads, for home. So they'd begin crying, then they'd remember and break off, afraid, and in the silence that followed you could hear a kind of *welling*: the anguished longing to cry and cry like any ordinary kid might do if he was homesick and lonely and bewildered. If you ask me the sound I remember most clearly from St Finbar's, then it's not the sound of the wind raving or the sea roaring or the bells that ruled our lives, it's that crying of the small kids in the dormitory upstairs. When I first heard it at the beginning of the year I'd expected someone would go up and calm them down, someone like John Rushall, perhaps, or even Father Stuckey. That didn't happen and as time passed I realised that, like the rule about not going back upstairs after breakfast, it was part of our training, our formation: for us there was no use crying because no one would ever come to comfort us. Like soldiers, we were being taught to have no pity for ourselves, and even then the edge of it struck me: that if you had no pity on yourself, how could you have it for other people, ever?

One night of bitter cold, the crying from upstairs was so loud you could hear it above the shrieking and the rattling of the wind. Frankie and I lay listening—it was impossible to sleep. We didn't talk; he always went quiet when the kids were crying, though I could hear his body shifting restlessly on his bed. Then a child cried out suddenly, 'Mummy! Oh Mummy!' and then, remembering sharply where he was and what he was supposed to be, he changed it quickly to, 'Mary! Oh Mary!' A boy with a deeper voice was sobbing wordlessly.

I heard the creak of Frankie's bed, the scrape of his door across the floor, quick determined steps passing my room and heading towards the stairs, up to that cold dormitory beneath the tower where on the windy nights of feast days they must have been able to hear the flag slapping cleanly way above their heads. I got up and went down the corridor towards the stairs. Frankie was already at the top and I thought he'd go in and start talking to the kids, calm them down; instead he stayed standing in the doorway and I pictured the rows of small faces turned curiously towards him, wondering why he didn't speak. Then, unexpectedly, he began to sing.

Hushabye, don't you cry,
Go to sleep, you little baby,

It was a lullabye, very soft and gentle, yet though Frankie's voice held a great tenderness, there was something hard in it too, hard and young and even angry, and you felt it was anger for everything that made them cry.

When you wake, you shall have cake,
And all the pretty little horses.

Outside the wind had dropped and the lullabye spilled out through the great spaces of the building, flooded down the stairs and along the corridors and passages, found its way into every distant room. I imagined Old Blinky listening, smiling sleepily, Father James and Father Gorman lifting their heads from their books, Father Stuckey scratching his head and wondering, 'Now, what's that?' I saw the Rector starting from some shallow snore-filled sleep, reaching for his dressing gown, his face already congested with rage. And of course there was Etta—he would be at his desk still, bent over the Book of Little Things. He would recognise Frankie's voice and his lips would move into that thin straight line, which in him might have passed for a smile. In a moment, when he'd completed the sentence he'd been working on, he'd get up from his chair and walk to the door. The Rector would come rushing from his room, and all the other teachers and the prefects in a crowd behind him; in a moment there'd be the sound of doors flying open and running feet... I stood there gripping the banister and I thought how this was it at last: it was all over for Frankie now, in the morning he'd be gone.

Upstairs he was still singing.

I didn't go back to my room. I stood there and waited for them to come. Only they didn't. Nothing I'd imagined happened. Even Etta didn't appear. The small boys were quiet now. Frankie finished his lullabye and came down to his room again. I was standing in the corner of the landing and he walked right past without even seeing me, and after a bit, when I was absolutely sure no one was going to come, I went into my own room and got back into bed. Next door Frankie was quiet, already asleep. There was a strange beautiful hush over the whole great building and I swear there was a kind of warmth in it, I could feel it on my face and in the air. In the morning no one said a word about the incident, except now and then I'd see an awed face turned in Frankie's direction as he walked by.

He'd got away with it, and I didn't for a second know how.

*

'Well, they'd have thought it was nice, you know,' Miri said to me once when we talked about that night. 'Your teachers.'

'Nice? They didn't think in terms of nice, Miri.'

She laughed. 'Oh, I bet some of them did. I bet Father Stuckey did.'

'Yes, I suppose he might have.' Father Stuckey left the priesthood a few years after I was ordained. He married a nurse and they went to live in Perth, where they had four children, all boys. I imagine him with these boys on long summer evenings, out on an oval like the one across the road from my house, teaching them to bat and bowl. On the first day of a new season they'd have a bright new ball and Mr Stuckey would throw it high up in the air and shout, 'To the glory of God!', embarrassing them all. And sometimes, very occasionally, he'd stop what he was doing and stand very still and quiet, his big face turned up towards the sky. 'Dad?' the boys would clamour, tugging at his shirt, 'Dad, what's up?' And then in a moment he'd be all right again, and they'd get on with the game.

'The Rector wouldn't have thought it was nice,' I said to Miri. 'Frankie sang that lullabye in the middle of the Great Silence, remember? They were strict about that at St Finbar's. There was this story they read us from *The Science of Saints*—'

'*The Science of Saints*! I don't believe you!'

'It's true. It was one of the books we had for the readings at mealtimes. And there was a story where this nun fell down the stairs in the middle of the night and broke her leg, and lay there until the next morning because she didn't want to call out and break the Great Silence.'

Miri made a snorting sound.

'Yes,' I said, 'even I didn't quite believe that story. All the same, the Rector wouldn't have thought a song in the middle of the Great Silence was nice at all, even if it was a lullabye. I'd have expected him to come crashing out, roaring.'

'Didn't you say it was very cold? And he was all warm and tucked up in bed—'

'You're such a cynic, Miri.'

'And you're such a romantic, Tom.'

'The cold wouldn't have bothered Etta, though. I still can't understand why he didn't come.'

'He'd have noticed the Rector and the teachers weren't reacting; he'd have guessed then that they were going to let it go. And so he had to let it go too. He must have been furious.'

'It was hard to tell what he felt. Always.'

The next morning at breakfast I glanced towards the Seniors' table: whatever Etta felt, he looked just as usual, aloof and sedate. He was buttering a slice of toast and then cutting it neatly into four exact squares.

'And he was only a kid, after all,' said Miri with a little sigh.

'What? WHAT?'

'He was only a kid, Tom. Remember how you told me he entered St Finbar's at ten? The course was five years, wasn't it? Before the Senior Seminary? He was head prefect, but he wouldn't have been more than fifteen. Think of it, Tom! He was younger than you.'

Her words shook me. I didn't want to think of it, that Etta was only a child.

'There was nothing young about him, ever,' I said.

*

It was true that Etta had seemed ageless to us back then. Perhaps that's why we were so surprised when his parents came to visit. It was about a week after the lullabye incident, and we saw the big grey car parked in the courtyard as we came out from lunch. Most visiting parents were excluded from the building, even those who'd travelled hundreds of miles, sitting up all night in dusty railway carriages—they were not special, they were not given to God as our teachers were, as we would be some day. They waited humbly in the courtyard while their child was brought to them, and they were allowed to spend a few hours with him down behind the dairy, where a stretch of ground had been asphalted over and furnished with a couple of rough wooden tables and some benches. They brought picnics—pies and cakes and soft drinks they'd bought from the shops down in Shoreham.

Because of their status (Etta's father was a High Court judge, there were bishops on both sides of the family) Etta's parents were allowed inside, as mine had been because my father was an old friend of Father James. From the windows of the library later that afternoon we saw a man and woman emerge from the main door with the Rector, Etta walking a few steps behind. The man was tall and grey-haired. He had a priestly look about him, a thin, ascetic face with inward-looking eyes. The mother—'He's got a mother!' exclaimed Frankie—and yes, that was it, you didn't think of Etta having a mother because it was almost impossible to imagine him small and trusting, holding someone's hand. Here she was though: pale skin and dim brown hair, those same neat expressionless features and that queer gliding walk that made you think she was moving in another element than the one the rest of us breathed. They shook hands with the Rector, and then Etta accompanied them to the big grey car. Again he walked a few steps behind them, as if his rank was lower. There were no hugs and kisses, only another cool handshake, and when the car started we didn't see them wave.

Etta didn't wave either. Before the car reached the gates he'd turned sharply and walked back inside. There was something almost military about his bearing; you half expected to hear the click of heels.

'He's not like us,' whispered Frankie. I supposed by 'not like us' he meant that Etta had no real feelings and wouldn't care in the least if his parents were cold to him—indeed, he might have thought it right and proper. But what I remember most clearly about that moment is the little rush of joy I felt at Frankie's use of the word 'us'—that he was including me with him. Almost, I squeezed his hand.

15.

My mother wrote to tell me that Miri was getting married in September and everyone was hoping I'd be able to come to the wedding.

I'd visited Miri's home in the Territory several times, and now a rush of memories flooded in: the airy old timber house with verandas all round, the sheds, the horses, the waterhole where you could swing into the water from a rope—I saw it all in a fever of longing. And my family! To see them all again: my mother and father, Aunty Sarah and Uncle Ray, Miri in her wedding dress—for a while I even daydreamed about taking Frankie with me, how he'd love it all! I knew it was impossible, even for me the Rector's permission was required.

He wouldn't give it. 'No, you can't,' he said. On the desk in front of him I saw a square envelope with silver wedding bells embossed in one corner and Miri's embroidery of kisses all round. The envelope was fat so I knew it contained a letter as well as the invitation card. So far she hadn't written to me at St Finbar's.

'I feel so sorry about that,' she told me later. 'I was in love, Tom, I was so in love with Chris. Love makes you selfish, and I was crazy about him. It was only when I sent you the invitation that I wrote a letter. And then when I heard you weren't allowed to come I sent you another one. It was the longest letter—'

'I didn't get it. I saw the first one though, the one that came with the invitation.'

There it sat on the Rector's desk, addressed to me. He didn't hand it over; instead he gave me a lecture on the love of God. I was here at St Finbar's to serve God, he told me, to learn to love Him, as He loved me. Families, friends—he paused a little on that last word, and I wondered if he meant Frankie, if he'd seen us together when he was patrolling the grounds and gardens, his small black eyes veering sharply from the pages of his breviary. I wondered too if Etta had made some kind of report. Close friendships were frowned on at St Finbar's, 'special friendships' they were called. Sometimes the friends were separated. I thought of being moved from my room, of Frankie being moved; I didn't know how I'd manage a whole night without the sound of his soft breathing from next door. It would be him they moved, and because he was always in trouble they might give him a room on the first floor, right next to the prefects' rooms, where Etta could watch him all the time. Perhaps the wall between their rooms would be as thin as ours was, and then it would be Etta who heard that soft breathing, his every shift and sigh.

'Are you listening to me, boy?'

'Yes.'

He glared.

'I mean, yes, Father.'

The vein in his forehead was throbbing, I could see he was in a bad mood. Perhaps if I'd asked him the next day I'd have got a different answer and been allowed to go to Miri's wedding. He was known to be changeable, on rare occasions he could even get jolly, though only for a little while.

'I saw him crying once,' Joey Gertler would tell me years later when we met at the Rector's funeral.

'Crying! When was that?'

'When I was at St Finbar's. It was late at night. I'd gone out walking, trying to get my mind off food. Frankie wasn't the only one who went wandering round, I reckon most of us did at some time or other. Anyway, I was passing the Rector's study and I looked in, and there he was, sitting in his big chair, bawling his eyes out. Great big fat tears they were, like a little kid's. But the thing that got me was the shoes—'

'The shoes?'

'Great big shiny ones. They looked—it sounds weird, I know, but they looked sort of—blameless. Not that he was, by any means—except they got to me, those shoes. When I came back from my wander his light was out and I thought of him lying in bed, that big head of his flat on the pillow, and I wondered what he thought about. How old was I then? Fifteen? I suppose it was the first time I actually realised adults were human, like we were.'

That afternoon when the Rector refused me permission to go to Miri's wedding, there was no sign of humanity that I could see. Families and friends were distractions, he repeated, and I seemed to be particularly susceptible, I must learn to do without these affections and concentrate on the love of God.

'The love of God!' he thundered, thumping his huge fist on the desk, so that Miri's letter jumped and our eyes went to it and his fleshy fingers closed over the envelope and he slid it into a drawer. 'That's mine,' I whispered. He didn't hear. 'The love of God!' he roared again. 'That's the important thing!' His cheeks mottled with a strange colour that was more purple than red. He dismissed me.

Dazed, I walked away down the corridor. My thoughts were like a baby's, simple and insistent: I want to go! I want to go! I want to go! Tears welled in my eyes. My head cleared as I walked out into the courtyard and then I began wondering, what was the love of God? What did it mean? They never told you, not in any way you could understand. And why was it wrong to love your family, anyway? If you weren't allowed to love people, what kind of person would you be?

The love of God—once I'd thought I knew what this phrase meant. I'd heard it all my life, in school and church; I'd taken it for granted that God loved us. What kind of love was God's? What was love anyway? I thought of my mother bandaging my father's hand in the kitchen that night before I went away. I thought of Den and Joseph playing the board game in their living room that rainy night when Dad and I were driving home from the camp. Frankie's face flickered for a moment behind my eyes.

When I left the Rector's study it was only halfway through the recreation period. As I came out through the cloisters I could see the kids playing football over in the paddock; Frankie didn't seem to be amongst them, but I spotted Etta at once. He wasn't on the field—he had some kind of exemption from sport—he was standing beneath the trees at the end of the pitch and he was staring up the hillside towards the wall. I could see no sign of Frankie up there, no flash of red sweater against the drab grey-greens, yet Etta kept on staring and I guessed he'd seen me coming and wanted me to understand that he knew all about Frankie going up the hill and looking down through the wall at the St Brigid's girls. He wanted to scare me, I think, and to gloat; though he didn't actually look at me there was something slightly triumphant about the very way he held that big domed head. And for a long while the two of us stood there silently, Etta's pale eyes fixed on the wall, my own eyes on Etta. Then I turned away.

I saw Father Stuckey standing in the long grass of the paddock next to the cricket oval. He was all by himself so I went over. He looked up and smiled when he saw me coming; he had a muddy old cricket ball in his hand. 'Found this in the grass here,' he explained, holding it up for me to see. His voice held true delight, the ball might have been the kind of gold nugget you only found in museums. Though he was mad about any kind of sport, cricket was his favourite; the older kids said he'd been a hopeful for the state before he came to St Finbar's. 'Must've been left over from last season,' he went on, picking at the mud around the ball's seams and then rubbing it up and down the front of his cassock to get it clean. The cassock was a mess, you could see what he'd had for breakfast on it, and all last week's meals, and now smears of mud and grass were being added. I thought of him in the Rector's study, standing hangdog, being yelled at for untidiness and letting down the side.

'Father,' I said. 'What's the love of God?'

His hand went still and all the cheerfulness drained from his face and I wished I'd never asked him and spoiled his delight in finding the cricket ball. I wanted to say 'sorry' and walk away, only it was too late now. Besides, I really needed to know and somehow I thought it was Father Stuckey, rather than the older ones, who might be able to tell me, in ordinary words from the ordinary world. 'God's love of us, I mean,' I added. 'Not our love of God.'

'Ah.' He studied the ball closely, picking at a stubborn fleck of mud. 'God's love,' he said, and sighed, his eyes drifting towards the edge of the paddock. 'God's love.' He drew in a breath; it was a deep one and you pictured his big pink lungs taking in the air like a diver high up on the edge of a board. 'Well, we Christians follow the God revealed in Jesus, right?'

'Yes.'

'And Jesus taught that God was a loving father, didn't he? Like the father in the story of the prodigal son?'

'Yes.' My heart had sunk already.

He smiled at me, encouraging. 'Like your own father, perhaps.'

I thought of my father in the free surgery he held on Thursday afternoons. It was mostly the women from the army camp who came, and my father would sit beside them on the sofa he kept in the consulting room, his head bowed, listening silently to their stories. Sometimes they'd be crying. When they'd gone he'd stand at the window watching them walk away along the street. If God's love was some heavenly version of this, we'd all be okay. If God's love was like that of Frankie's father, we were done for.

'God *is* love,' Father Stuckey was saying. 'For God so loved the world that he gave his only son, that whosoever believes in him shall not perish, but have everlasting life.'

The familiar words had no effect; instead a feeling of sternness rose up inside me, as if Father Stuckey was telling lies.

He waved his hand towards the gardens and the playing fields, the boys in their old sweaters pouring down towards the goal. 'That's God's love.'

I could think of nothing to reply.

'That help?' He inclined his big head towards me. I could see the hope in his eyes. The kindness.

'Mmm.' I remembered the sense I used to have of the gentle hand above my head and the wonderful feeling of lightness it had given, as if every part of me was truly alive and meant to be.

'Is God lightness?'

He beamed. 'Of course! Of course He is! Doesn't John say so? "Light is come into the world."'

He hadn't understood what I'd meant. Despite the kindness he was like the others: I had a dull feeling that you could talk to them for a hundred years and they'd never understand you and you'd never understand them.

'Okay?' he asked.

'Yes, Father. Thank you.'

'What I'm here for.' He held the ball up and smiled. 'Good as new!' he said, and then he tossed it high up into the air and shouted, 'To the glory of God!'

As I left him and made my way towards the main building, twilight was falling, the bleak grey twilight of a winter's day. Kids were trailing back in groups from the football and the handball courts; there was still no sign of Frankie. As I passed the teachers' rooms a face loomed up suddenly in one of the windows, a hand beckoned me inside. It was Father James. Reluctantly, I went into his room and sat in the chair he offered. He told me—news travelled fast at St Finbar's—that he'd heard I'd been refused permission to attend my cousin's wedding.

'Yes.' I looked down at the floor. His words brought the disappointment rushing back at me: the whole happy day I'd be missing, the sun shining, Miri in her wedding dress and Chris beside her, bridesmaids, Mum and Dad and everyone—and as if she'd been right there next to me, I heard Miri's laughing voice say, 'See? Now if you hadn't gone off to St Finbar's, I'd have thrown you the bouquet!'

'I'm sorry about that,' murmured Father James. The Rector wasn't mentioned, it was as if the refusal had nothing to do with St Finbar's, had come drifting down, all by itself, out of a clear blue sky. 'I'm sorry,' he said again and made a vague sifting gesture with his hands, adding with a little sigh, 'But that's our life in God.'

The same cold severity I'd felt when Father Stuckey had quoted the words of the gospel took hold of me. Why was it? I wanted to ask him. Why was it our life in God to miss a cousin's wedding?

He was staring at me. 'How are things otherwise?' he asked.

'Fine,' I answered. 'Everything's fine.'

'That's good to hear.' He rubbed his hands together and I had a sense that there were lots of things he'd like to tell me only he didn't dare, and that's why we were sitting here with nothing much to say.

There was a book lying on the edge of the desk and I read its title: *The Ministry of Fear*. It made me think of the way we all held our breaths when someone dropped a fork at dinner and the vein in the Rector's forehead began to throb; how people whispered about Etta having a thousand eyes, and how wherever you went at St Finbar's you felt someone was watching; and how anything you said might somehow turn out to be wrong. The ministry of fear—that was us. Frankie was the only one who wasn't afraid. And as if that thought had conjured him, outside the window Frankie appeared on the path beside the teachers' garden. That severe last light which seemed to drain the colour out of everything else made his hair and sweater almost luminous.

Father James turned to see what I was looking at. 'Ah, your friend,' he said, and we both watched as Frankie crossed to the garden tap and bent to drink. Then he lifted his head and wiped his mouth with the back of his hand and sauntered slowly towards the library.

'You know, when he came, your friend, I mean—' he paused, glancing towards the window, seeming to wait for me to say something, and when I didn't, he went on, 'Yes, when he came we gave him that room next to yours because we thought you'd be a good influence.' He smiled, inviting confidences, and again when I said nothing he went on. 'A restraining influence, we thought. Perhaps even a force for change.'

Change. I thought of Frankie's warmth and generosity, his delight in the loveliness of the world. I thought of him handing the oranges out in that cold little yard, singing to the kids in the dormitory—*Hushabye, don't you cry*— It was true that he always broke the rules, yet I thought most of the things he did were good in a way that was larger than the world the rest of us inhabited: the world of that little green rule book we carried in our pockets.

'You wouldn't be able to,' I said.

'What?'

'You wouldn't be able to change him. And—' I tried to hold it back, but I couldn't keep the anger from my voice. 'And you *shouldn't.*'

He looked at me in surprise.

'If you knew what he was like, really, then you wouldn't want to change him.'

He leaned forward across the desk. 'What is he like, Tom?'

'He's a good person. He's *good*.'

'Ah.' He picked up a pencil from the desk and studied it for a moment, then he put it down again and it rolled, and we both sat there watching it, silently. When it stopped, a finger's breadth from the edge, he asked, 'Do you know what St Thomas Aquinas says about the good?'

I shook my head.

He reached for the pencil again and rolled it between his palms. 'St Thomas says, *The good is what all things desire.*'

I don't think for a moment that he meant anything by it; I don't think he meant to hint that I desired Frankie, that my feelings for him were sexual. We were all more innocent in those days, ignorant, perhaps. He meant only that this, literally, was the way Thomas Aquinas spoke about the good. And I don't think I knew then, not consciously anyway, that what I felt for Frankie was desire, though the word itself sent a funny little shiver down my spine—the kind you get when you hear a certain bar of music, or a perfect line of poetry. All the same I made some excuse about being late for evening study and got up quickly from my chair. I didn't want to sit there any longer talking about Frankie, it made me feel like a spy.

I went outside and stood for a moment in the porch. The wind had got up while I was inside, howling and rattling things about.

That's why Etta didn't hear me. He was bent over the tap where Frankie had been drinking.

He must have been following him, following at a distance, quietly. He'd hidden himself when Frankie had gone to the tap and from his hiding place he'd watched him drinking, and when Frankie had gone he'd slipped out and drunk from the tap himself. Concealed in the shadows of the porch I watched him; in that deepening twilight, his close-shorn head and the way he was stooped over made him appear like an old man. His colourless lips covered the place where Frankie's own lips had been. He straightened and I stepped back further into the shadows. I didn't need to, he couldn't see me, he might as well have been blind. His eyes were closed, his face turned upwards, giving him the look of some love-struck saint in ecstasy. He raised one of those neat little paws and pressed a finger against his lips, as if sealing something there; the gesture had reverence, as if what he sealed there was sacred. And again that shiver ran through me, as if my body took in something my mind couldn't grasp, not yet.

A bell rang. I began to run towards the library. Halfway there I turned and looked back and in the deepening dusk I could just make out his small dark shape, one hand pressed to his mouth, still standing there.

16.

Hay Jarrell's mum and dad came to see him. Theirs was a very different visit from that of Etta's parents. The Jarrells were poor. They had no car and would have travelled almost eight hundred miles on trains and buses. They came walking up the hill, Mr Jarrell carrying a big string bag full of the picnic food they'd bought to eat with Hay at those wooden tables behind the old dairy. Later that afternoon Frankie and I were with a work party clearing young saplings from the high bank above the driveway and we saw the Jarrells leaving, walking down the drive towards the gates. Hay was still with them and as they passed below us on the road he looked up and saw us and whispered something to his mum and dad. I suppose he'd told them about the lullabye and the time Frankie had torn off the piece of his shirt to make a hanky, because Mr Jarrell smiled and gave us a little wave and Mrs Jarrell blew Frankie a kiss. He was delighted. It was like that time the dentist's nurse had kissed him; he touched the centre of his cheek, as if a real kiss had actually landed there.

But when they reached the gates Mrs Jarrell was crying. She held Hay close, his face pressed up against her blue woolly cardigan. She was small like him. Beside me Frankie was watching them, hungrily, as if he could never get enough of the way Mrs Jarrell's thin arms curved close around Hay's skinny body, and how one freckled hand stroked her son's narrow back, up and down and up and down. And how Mr Jarrell, who didn't look the least like them, who was tall and gawky with a big plain face, stood up close and his huge farmer's hand rested on top of Hay's head and covered all of it. Frankie took it all in and I noticed how the longing on his face was different from the longing I'd seen that time up on the hillside when he was staring down at Bella in the St Brigid's garden. There'd been a kind of happy confidence then, like he knew in his heart that if he'd been out in the ordinary world, Bella would have wanted him. When he looked at the Jarrells with Hay there was none of that confidence, only a sort of sadness, so you guessed he'd wanted that kind of love when he was little, and he hadn't got it and now it was too late. The bell rang and we picked up our tools and went back to the garden sheds, and all the way Frankie walked beside me quietly, his head down.

*

Later we heard that when Hay's mum and dad walked away down the hill, Hay had stayed by the gates and they'd kept turning round to wave. Long after they were out of sight he was standing there watching the empty road as if he had a hope they might come back. He stood there all through the afternoon until it started to get dark, and then John Rushall came and led him gently away. I don't know who saw all this—that was the way of things at St Finbar's: word got round and you never knew quite where it came from or whether it was true or not—but from what we saw that afternoon on the bank above the driveway, I'm sure that particular story was true.

'Did you see how they loved him?' Frankie asked me that night. 'Hay's mum and dad? Did you see?'

'Yeah,' I said, and he fell asleep at once and I fell asleep too. I dreamed of St Thomas Aquinas. I dreamed he was sitting on my bed. In all the years since I've never had a dream so real: my room exactly as it was when I'd closed my eyes, right down to the single sock lying in the middle of the floor, only now there was the peculiar warm heaviness of another person sitting close to me, beside my legs. He wore a long gold robe which was pleated at the top and seemed to be made of silk. His face, so bland and chubby in the portrait which hung in our library, now looked old and sad and I thought he was going to say that thing Father James had told us the night Frankie had kissed the portrait of the Archbishop: how after his vision, everything he'd written seemed like straw in the wind. Instead he spoke those other words Father James had quoted to me: 'The good is what all things desire,' and again the very sound of that word—desire—sent the strange, sweet shiver right through me. 'Why?' I asked St Thomas. 'Why do I feel like that?' and he held out his long narrow hand and then I woke and he was gone. The dream had been so real that it took me a while to realise that's all it had been, that I was awake now and nothing had happened and I was lying in my bed the same as any ordinary night with Frankie asleep on the other side of the partition.

Only it wasn't the same. Instead of Frankie's soft breathing I could hear a strange sound coming from his room: a regular rhythmic sound, a little *snick* and then a long smooth *shirrr*, like scissors running through a length of cloth. Then a long silence, so long I thought the noise had stopped and whatever was making it had gone, only then it began again: *Snick! Shirrr*—

I went out into the corridor and stood close to Frankie's door. It was much thicker than the partition between our rooms and I couldn't hear anything. 'Frankie?' I whispered. There was no reply. I grasped the doorknob and turned it slowly.

I don't know what I thought I would find in there. The strange sound had unnerved me, and remnants of my dream still hung about: St Thomas's sad face, his long white hand stretched out to me, those words which seemed so mysterious: *The good is what all things desire.* Out in the corridor the silence was so intense that for once I'd have been glad to hear one of the kids upstairs cry out—at least that sound was familiar and human, it wasn't part of a dream about a man who'd died almost seven hundred years ago. I stood outside that door and I thought how anything might be behind it. I wouldn't have been surprised to find Etta sitting on Frankie's bed, his face raised in a sly, knowing stare. I pushed the door open.

It's well over fifty years now, yet I only have to close my eyes and I can see that room: the dark night pressing against the high slit of window, the big shadows from Frankie's torch looming on the walls. His bed was empty, the blanket thrown back, a pair of scissors lay on the sheet and the empty covers of two of the rough workbooks we used at St Finbar's. Frankie was sitting at the desk, his back to me, writing. He'd taken the pages from the workbooks and then cut them into smaller squares—*Snick! Shirrrr*—that was the sound I'd heard. A neat stack of them lay on the desk beside him.

I closed the door softly. 'Frankie?'

He looked round.

'What are you doing?'

In answer he pointed to the stack of small sheets on the desk. I picked the top one up. Written in the centre were the words: *Bella—my beautiful, beautiful Bella, I love you. Frankie Maguire.* The word 'love' seemed bigger than the others, though I knew this might have been an illusion— it simply struck harder. I leafed through the rest of the little sheets—the message was the same on every one.

'I was dreaming of her,' he said, 'and then I woke up and— oh, I don't know—I wanted to write down how I felt. Only I'm not very good at writing things, so there's only that.' He ran a hand though his hair. The soft buttery strands seemed to pour through his fingers. 'They're love letters, sort of—little ones. I guess they say the most important thing.'

'There's so many.'

'Yes, I know. Once I started I couldn't stop.'

I put the love letters back on the desk. 'What're you going to do with them?'

'Just keep them with me. To look at, I suppose, every now and then.'

He saw my bewildered expression. 'Well, you've got to have *something*.'

I hated it when he said that. His cassock was hanging on the back of the chair and he picked up the love letters, divided them into two and tucked them into the long pockets on either side. The torchlight caught his face and I noticed how it had become thinner, the cheekbones more prominent. Above them his eyes seemed more beautiful than ever, luminous in the half dark. I wished he could have had parents like Hay's, or mine. His father thought he was scum. His mother—he hardly ever spoke of her, there was only that one time when she'd found out about Manda Sutton and said she was too ashamed to say her prayers. That didn't mean she didn't love him; perhaps she was the one who'd taught him the lullabye. 'You know that lullabye you sang for the kids upstairs? Did your mother use to sing that to you?'

'What?'

'The lullabye. Did your mother sing it?'

'Mum didn't sing.'

Something terrible happened then. He looked straight at me, though there was a kind of blindness, a glaze in his stare.

And when he spoke his voice was changed, it was tense and full of hisses, it seemed to fizz. I could hardly take in what I heard. 'Get away from me,' he spat. 'Get away, I'm sick of the sight of you!'

I'd been standing right next to the desk and I jumped back, stricken.

'Oh!' he gasped, jumping up from the chair. The awful voice had gone. 'Not you, Tom, I didn't mean you! How could you ever think I meant you?'

I shook my head and sat down on the bed. I was shaking.

He came and sat beside me. 'It was my mum,' he said. 'That's who I meant. That's how she used to go when we were all hanging round her and she was trying to get the tea.'

'It sounds horrible,' I whispered, and he looked at me in surprise.

'She didn't mean it; we got on her nerves sometimes.'

He crawled in under the blanket and lay down, his arms behind his head. I could feel his long legs against my back, and I kept thinking of what his mum said and how it must have hurt when he was little, even if she didn't mean it. 'It isn't fair!' I wanted to shout. I learned a lot about love in those few months I spent with Frankie at St Finbar's, and that's what love is, I think: feeling another's pain and sorrow as if it was your own.

'There were too many of us, that's all,' Frankie sighed, excusing her. 'She got really tired sometimes.' He took his arms from beneath his head and slid them down under the blankets.

His eyes closed. 'Anyway, all that stuff back home, it doesn't matter now.'

'Why doesn't it?'

'Because I've got Bella now.'

There was something queerly exalted in the way he said this. It was weird, and instead of feeling jealous like I often did when he talked about Bella, I felt uncomfortable, even a little scared. I must have been staring because he said, 'No, don't look at me like that. I'm not crazy, honest. I'm not going to do anything, I haven't *been* doing anything. I'm not going down there and asking her out, honest I'm not. Fat chance!' He studied me silently for a moment. 'You thought I was, didn't you?'

'No, no, I didn't,' I mumbled, my face turning red.

'I won't,' he said. 'I promised, didn't I?'

I didn't answer, and he repeated, 'Didn't I?'

'Yes.'

'All I mean is: I've got her to think about. It helps.' He flung himself back on the pillow and said that thing I hated again. 'You've got to have *something*,' and I wanted to say, 'You've got me,' only I didn't, of course. Instead I said, 'Goodnight, Frankie,' and my voice went low and soft on his name, like a lullabye, and then I got up and went back to my room.

17.

He was right, you had to have something. Except it didn't seem fair that the mere thought of Bella could mean so much to him—that without knowing or understanding him in the least, simply by existing, carelessly, she could comfort him. I puzzled over his promise that he 'wasn't going to do anything'. I knew he meant it; I also knew he wasn't the kind of person who'd be content with simply thinking and dreaming. He wasn't like me—perhaps that was why I liked him so much, the difference held a kind of glamour. I remembered how on his way to St Finbar's, missing the train in that small country town, he'd so quickly become part of the stationmaster's family, a part of the town. He'd got to know the shopkeepers and their families and become friendly with the old men who sat on the bench outside the post office every day—one of them had taught him how to make a box kite. He always needed to be part of the world; if he fell in love, how could he ever be content with love letters that stayed in his pocket and never went anywhere?

So I wasn't a bit surprised when after a few minutes I heard him go out.

I waited a little while and then followed him. As I came out the door he was already on the far side of the courtyard and I could tell from the direction that he was heading for the hillside. By the time I reached the paddock he was already out of sight. It seems odd now to think how I never once thought of Etta as I hurried after Frankie, never thought of him following us, or hiding, watching, in the trees. I think this sudden forgetfulness, which was like a kind of freedom, had something to do with the strangeness of that night: the dream of St Thomas sitting on my bed, which had seemed so completely real, the eerie noise of scissors on paper that I'd heard from Frankie's room, the little love letters, the strange exalted way in which Frankie had said, 'I've got Bella now.' Then halfway up the hill the moon slid from behind a cloud, a huge bright sickle like a sword hanging in the sky, and if Etta had so much as crossed my mind I think I'd have dismissed him as nothing more than an overzealous prefect who simply wanted to bring Frankie into line. But I didn't think of him at all, though I know now that he was watching us that night. Of course he was. He saw everything.

When I caught up with Frankie at the top of the hill he looked pleased to see me, as if he wanted company. I think that glimpse of Hay with his parents had unsettled him deeply, made him needy in some way he hardly recognised. It may even have been the reason he wrote those love letters he could never send. And there was nothing for him up there on the hill; the garden and the school were all in darkness, the moon on the long windows gave them a dull silvery gleam, like two rows of big metal trays washed and stood on end to dry.

It was windy and bitterly cold. As we stood there a light came on in the upper storey of St Brigid's. The window was uncurtained and the room inside it, plain as ours, lit so brilliantly that each item of furniture showed clearly: the big desk with its four straight-backed wooden chairs, the skinny grey cupboard, the bookshelf along one wall. Beside me I heard Frankie draw in his breath and I knew he was hoping for the miracle to occur and Bella to walk into that room. She didn't, of course; it was an elderly woman with close-cropped hair who stood in the doorway, looking round the room. She wore a dark-green dressing gown and her movements were so slow and bewildered that I guessed she'd been unable to sleep, that she'd been lying in bed for a long time, awake and thinking. She crossed the room to the shelves and took down a book, riffled for a moment through the pages, then put it back on the shelf and left the room. The light went out. There was something so painfully dreary about this little scene—the starkness of the room, the elderly woman, the very antithesis of Bella with her springy black curls and brilliant smile, that you felt the very heart go out of you.

'It's a kind of blasphemy,' said Frankie suddenly.

'What is?'

'Formation.'

Formation was the name given to our education, our training to be priests. It was such a hard, ungiving word: it always made me think of the shiny instruments in my father's surgery.

'God made us, didn't he?' demanded Frankie angrily. 'He *formed* us, so St Finbar's can't *re-form* us, can they? They can't go and make us different from what God did!' He kicked at a stone and a kind of chime rang out, thin and metallic in the freezing air, and that too sounded so desolate that something inside you seemed to clench itself protectively, your heart perhaps, even your very life. With an abrupt movement Frankie swung round and pointed down the hill towards the great building of the seminary huddled like some huge frozen animal at the bottom of the hill. 'They might as well cut our balls off!' he cried. 'They might as well!' His voice was so clear that I half expected lights to spring up in the windows of the school and seminary. His shoulders were shaking. I reached a hand towards him and he backed away, straightening his whole body, shaking his head. 'No, I'm all right, I'm all right. I'm okay.' He turned back and stared down at St Brigid's. 'It's all dreams anyway, me and Bella. Being in love with her. You can't keep on being in love with a girl if there's nothing you can *do*. I don't even know why I came up here.' He shoved his hands in his pockets and dragged out fistfuls of the love letters, ripping them, scrunching them, tossing them away from him. The wind caught and blew them onto bushes, sent them scuttling over the stones and grass and up against the wall. One flew into the gap, I caught it just before it sailed down onto the road. They had his name on them—quickly, I began to gather up the others, and after a few moments Frankie stooped and began to help. His long fingers moved quickly, so close to mine it seemed they would touch, yet somehow they never did. The words on the letters kept jumping up at me, *I love you, I love you,* sharp in the light from that sickle moon. There couldn't have been more than thirty, but the words seemed to strike at me a hundred, a thousand times.

When my father was dying I used to read to him. My mother had gone years before. He kept on loving her. 'Catullus,' he'd say to me, smiling, and I'd take the worn volume down from the shelves and read his favourite poem:

> *Give me a thousand kisses, and then a hundred,*
> *Then another thousand, then a second hundred*

And as I read I'd see those little white notes of Frankie's lying on the grass of that frozen hillside and the words leaping up at me and those long brown fingers so close to mine.

> *Give me a thousand kisses, then a hundred,*
> *Then another thousand, then a second hundred,*
> *Then yet another thousand, then a hundred…*

When all the love letters were gathered up, we turned back towards the seminary. Halfway down the hill Frankie stopped and I stopped and he asked me, 'Tom, have you ever had a girl?' I knew he didn't mean taking a girl out, going to the pictures, walking home with her and giving her a kiss at the door—he meant sex like he'd had with Manda Sutton.

'No.'

'I wish you had,' he said sadly, 'I wish you had.' Those brilliant eyes searched my face. 'How old are you?'

'Sixteen.'

He sighed. 'Sweet sixteen and never been kissed.'

'What?' I felt myself blushing again and hoped it was too dark for him to notice.

'It's just something my dad used to say, when my sisters turned sixteen, on their birthdays, he used to bawl out, "Sweet sixteen and never been kissed!" And then he'd give them this great whacking big kiss—mwaaa! They hated it. My biggest sister, Polly, she ran off when I was little; I don't know what happened to her, we never heard or anything. I can hardly remember her but I hope she gets lots of kisses wherever she is.' He shook his head. 'Sixteen. We'll be like that forever now.'

'How do you mean?'

'We'll be sweet sixteen for always, see? No more kisses. Not *proper* kisses, anyway—just those little old ladies who come up after mass and say, "Thank you, Father," and then they'll stand on tippy-toe and make their mouths like this—' he pleated his lips into a tiny shape, 'and give us this tiny little peck, like a birdie at a seed bell.'

'You could always leave.' The words sprang out of me, I could hardly believe I was saying them. I didn't want him to leave, of course I didn't! I'd worried for months that Etta would get him chucked out, sent away. Yet I did say them, I *had* to, there was this kind of *welling* in his voice, like the little kids upstairs when they were trying not to cry.

The effect on him was startling. 'Oh, no!' he whispered. 'Oh, no!' He stopped dead, his hands fell to his sides, the honest moon showed the shock on his face. 'Leave? I'd never leave! I *promised*!' And he glanced up at the sky.

I'd always known that his belief in heavenly beings was different to mine; now I heard in that astonished voice how close they were to him, like real people in the house next door. Like family. 'I'd *never* leave!' he repeated, and now there was a kind of rapture on his face that for a shocking moment reminded me of Etta standing by the tap in the teachers' garden, his face uplifted—

'I'm sorry,' I said quickly. 'Sorry. I just—I don't know why I said it. I shouldn't have.'

'That's okay.' He made a little gesture with his hand. 'That's just how it is with me,' he said, and then, quite unexpectedly, he smiled. 'Anyway, if I left I'd have no place to go. Dad'd kill me if I went back there. Homeless, I'd be.'

'You could stay at my place. My parents wouldn't mind. They like having people—' The idea of it surged up in me: Frankie living in my house, in the room down the hall from mine, I could see him in the holidays, perhaps I would also leave, perhaps I should, because I didn't understand the love of God. He'd taken his hand from my head, I felt angry so much of the time...

'No, it's okay,' Frankie was saying. 'But thanks. Thanks,

Tom. But see, I've got to stay. That promise was serious. Really.'

He leaned forward and kissed me on the lips. It was only friendship, perhaps a bit of gratitude, I knew that, just as I knew with that kiss that I loved him quite differently. Properly, I would say. Like my father loved my mother, or Denny loved Joseph. Perhaps I'd always known.

'You knew and you didn't know,' said Miri when I told her. She poked a finger in my chest. 'You knew in *there*.'

'The heart's on the left side,' I told her.

'And the heart *knows*.'

Whatever the heart knows, dear Miri, I felt no shock at the realisation of my love, simply an immense joy, so intense that I can't remember—no, I have no memory of it at all—the two of us walking across the paddock and through the gardens and the cloister and in through the door and up the stairs to our separate rooms. When I got into bed I remember sliding down beneath the blanket and the knowledge that I loved Frankie got in beside me like a person made of dreams and I took him in my arms.

'Goodnight, Tom.' The real Frankie's voice came from behind the wall, unselfconscious, the same as ever. I knew he wasn't like me. I knew it was girls he liked and he could never love me in that way. He'd have forgotten all about that kiss before we even reached the courtyard—and yet I was happy that night, happier than I'd ever been. I put a finger to my lips and I swear I could feel the warmth from his lips still trembling on my own. I pressed gently with my fingertip to seal it in.

18.

I was still in a daze at dinnertime the next evening. The whole day—chapel and classes and meals and sport—all of it had passed in a sort of fog. Only the brief glimpses of Frankie were clear: in front of me at chapel, two tables across at breakfast, his brown hand reaching for the milk jug, a flash of red sweater on the oval at Father Stuckey's training session. At lunchtime I'd looked up and our eyes had met across the tables and he'd smiled at me—the same smile as always. I've often wondered if he guessed about me; he was less innocent than I was, and although he came from a small town, he knew more about people and the world. I like to think he knew a gay boy when he saw one, even if the boy himself didn't know, and that—like my parents—it didn't matter to him; he liked you just the same, you were simply part of the lovely, lovely world. William Blake once wrote that everything that lives is holy and I think Frankie was a lot like him.

That evening in the refectory I underestimated Etta. Frankie's kiss and the realisation of my own nature had given me a kind of strength. 'It's being able to love another person, that's the most important thing,' my father had said, and I was able to love and I felt it made me a part of the world. I looked across at Etta standing at the head of the seniors' table; in the harsh light he looked weak and scrawny, the domed head too big for the spindly body, his pink baby's scalp shining through the close-shorn hair. I could hardly believe I'd been so afraid that this boy with his Book of Little Things had the power to separate me from Frankie.

So I had no suspicion of what was coming as the staff took their places at the high table. There was a conference in the city that evening so there were only three of them besides the Rector: Old Blinky, Father Stuckey and Father James. Grace was said: 'Bless, Lord, Your gifts in our use and ourselves in Your service, through Jesus Christ our Lord,' the Rector gabbled, so fast it all sounded like one word.

Amen. We all sat down except for Etta, who kept on standing. He tapped his glass again and picked up a single sheet of paper from the table—the list of readers. Except on feast days, talking at meals was forbidden, and selected students read from various devotional works. It was from one of these that I'd learned of the nun who'd broken her leg one night and, out of respect for the Great Silence, hadn't called for help till morning. For the last week our readings had been from *The Little Flowers of St Francis*. Etta looked down at his list and called out the name of the evening's reader. It was Hayden Jarrell.

Readings by the younger students were rare but not unknown; it had been one of the young ones, Johnny Lowry, who'd read the story of the stoical nun. Hay got to his feet, his small face flaming. 'M-me?' he stammered. Etta said nothing.

'Me?' asked Hay again. The Rector had been pouring a glass of wine, now he looked up and bellowed, 'Yes, boy, it's you! Now get a move on, we haven't got all night!'

His face still scarlet, Hay squeezed out along the narrow space between his table and the wall. His cassock was a little too long for him—his mother would have bought it a size too big, in the hope that he'd grow into it.

*

He did grow into it. I met him a few years back at the opening of a new college in the city, a tall willowy man in a grey suit that even I could see was expensive, still with that sandy hair which at St Finbar's had seemed to mirror all his terrors with its electric spikiness. Now it lay calm and smooth, streaked with a little grey. There was no trace of the stammer. We talked about Frankie, of course. 'You know, I'd never have thought he'd leave,' said Hay. 'He seemed like a stayer to me. And they didn't kick him out, even when he told the Rector off that time—' His cheeks coloured, remembering that night in the refectory. 'And that was my fault.'

'No, it wasn't. He'd have told the Rector off some day; you could see it coming. Always.'

Hay smiled. 'I'd take a guess it was the girls then. The reason for his leaving, I mean. You can tell when they like the girls. There's a kind of—glow to them. Frankie had it, and my Uncle Colly was just the same. I bet wherever Frankie is now, there'll be a girl. And she'll be beautiful.'

I was grateful to him for saying that. I was grateful whenever I met someone who believed Frankie was somewhere in the world.

*

That night in the refectory, as Hay scurried past the high table, the hem of his long cassock caught beneath his heel and he stumbled slightly. The Rector leaned forward and hissed at him. 'Pick up your feet, boy!'

Hoisting the hem well clear of his skinny ankles, Hay almost ran those last few steps to the lectern. He was so small his chin barely grazed the edge of its shelf and his fingers trembled as he grasped the silk ribbon that marked the place where last night's reader had finished. For a moment he simply stood there, silent, his small shoulders sagging in a dejected line—then the ribbon slipped from his hand and fell to the floor. He stooped and picked it up, then stood with it in his hand, staring blankly at the book. It was obvious he'd lost the place. Father Stuckey got up from his chair and walked round the edge of the table towards the lectern, where he turned a few pages and marked the place with the ribbon for Hay. 'The Wolf of Gubbio,' he whispered, patting him on the shoulder. Then he went back to the high table and sat down and the Rector looked up from his soup bowl and scowled at him.

'Of,' began Hay in his squeaky little kid's voice. '—of the most ho-ho-holy m-m-miracle of St Francis in t-t—'

On an ordinary day his stammer was barely noticeable. That evening of course wasn't ordinary: chosen unexpectedly, roared at by the Rector, forced to stand before us all and read, he could hardly form two words in succession. He would get a word and then stumble on the next, get a little rush of two or three, perhaps a whole sentence, and then stop altogether, his throat working—like a baby just learning to walk, you half expected him to fall down. Now and again he'd glance up from the book and look out at us and then he'd smile, and the smile was so pitiful that it gave you a shamed feeling, as if you were somehow to blame. We were having steamed pudding for dessert that night, and in the kitchen the helpers were already ladling it into the bowls and the smell of golden syrup seemed to hover over us in a thick sweet cloying smog. I've never been able to touch the stuff since. Hardly any of us were eating. The little kids sat frozen, their eyes fixed on Hay. At the seniors' table, John Rushall had laid his knife and fork across his plate and sat bolt upright, staring at the ceiling. Next to me Tim Vesey lifted a forkful of potato and gravy to his mouth and then put it down again. Only Etta seemed to be eating normally, knife and fork held neatly in those little paws. I looked across at Frankie's table and saw that he'd pushed his plate away and turned his chair round to face the lectern, his lips, his whole face, mouthing in silent encouragement, 'It's all right, you can do it, come on, Hay!'

Hay was too terrified to notice, he was blind to everything except the words on the page. Even when he looked up and smiled that dreadful frightened smile I'm sure he didn't really see us there. The silence in the refectory was so complete that you could actually hear him breathing, in and out and in and out, a hoarse ragged sound which seemed too old for him. It was then I glanced across at Etta.

He'd paused in his eating to take a sip of water from his glass. One sip, that was all. When he put the glass down on the table he picked up his napkin and wiped his lips, and then his gaze went straight to Frankie. I can't describe the expression on his face except to say that it reminded me of an empty thing filling, and that it terrified me because I saw I'd been right about him all along. John Rushall had been right, when he'd said, 'He gets these downs on people and then he wants to get rid of them, see?' And the kids had been right who whispered that Etta had a thousand eyes. He had set a last trap to get Frankie into trouble, and as the trap revealed itself to me I was both amazed and sickened to see how well Etta *knew* Frankie. From his watching, his *attention,* he knew Frankie as well as I did, as well as a mother might know her favourite child. He knew Frankie's sympathy and his protectiveness of the younger boys, he knew his impulsiveness, his fearlessness. He knew the Rector's temper and he would have noted Hay's stammer, and he put all these together and set up Hay Jarrell to read. He knew what would happen.

At the lectern, Hay was beginning again. 'St, St Francis, f-feeling great com-compass-com—'

Frankie edged further forward on his seat. 'Compassion,' he mouthed. In the silence the word seemed almost audible.

I knew the story of *The Wolf of Gubbio*. It had been a favourite of one of our teachers at primary school; she'd read it to us so many times that I knew bits off by heart. What struck me now was the gentleness of the story, where the wolf is forgiven and fed every day by the villagers until he dies of a peaceful old age—and how it seemed to belong to a world that was kindlier than ours. Up at the high table the Rector was eating, his thick fingers lifting the loaded forkfuls to his shiny lips, occasionally glancing contemptuously at Hay. Beside him Old Blinky seemed to have fallen into a doze, his head resting on one hand. These days I wonder about Old Blinky's dozes. He wasn't really old—in that photograph Frankie had found in the St Finbar's journal he looked roughly the same age as the Rector, who was only in his forties when he was Head at St Finbar's. I wonder now whether Blinky's dozes were really a form of hiding in tedious or difficult situations, pretending he wasn't there. Father Stuckey's broad face was flushed, he'd crumpled his table napkin into a round shape like a ball and was rubbing it against the front of his cassock. Father James wore his fine distant stare—perhaps he was thinking of my mother, or reflecting on those mysterious words of Aquinas: *The good is what all things desire.*

And Hay stumbled on, sentence after agonising sentence.

The students had been silent at first, embarrassed for him, even ashamed. Now after what seemed like an eternity of that stumbling voice, those tense silences when you thought he would never go on and the whole thing would never end, that we'd all be trapped in it forever like a spell, some of them began to jeer at him. The jeering was soft at first, an oddly delicate hissing, then a slow tapping of spoons began upon the tables, and someone called out, 'Hey! Hey! Hay!'

'Silence!' the Rector shouted. Father Stuckey stood up as if he was going to protest, then as suddenly sat down again, the balled napkin dropping from his hand. Hay clutched at his spiky hair.

There was the sudden raucous scrape of a chair across the stone floor. Frankie was on his feet and striding towards the high table. The table stood on a low dais and when he reached the edge he sprang up on it so that he stood only a few inches from the teachers' chairs. The Rector rose from his place. 'You!' he said slowly, ponderously. 'You dare—'

Frankie cut him off. I remember his voice as rather mild. 'Let him go,' he said, waving a hand towards the trembling Hay. 'Let him go back to his seat, please. I'll do the reading.'

'You will do *nothing*!' shouted the Rector, the vein jerking at his temple. '*You* will go back to your seat, and you will come to my study and see me after prayers!' He pointed at Hay. 'And that boy will continue with the reading.'

'No,' said Frankie, and a ripple of pure astonishment ran round the tables.

The Rector's heavy lips fell open in a wet red square. 'You defy me?'

For a moment Frankie said nothing. He stood with his head held slightly to one side, his eyes thoughtful, as if he was searching for the right words. 'It's wrong what you're doing,' he said. His gaze took in the pitiful figure of Hay at the lectern, swept back to the Rector. 'It's—' He paused, thoughtful again, looking for a second word.

'Frankie,' Father James whispered. 'Frankie—'

The Rector turned on him. 'And you shut up!' he bawled. There was a great gasp from all the tables.

'It's bad,' said Frankie, and this second simple word was wonderfully true.

The Rector's chest swelled out above the sash that girdled his soutane, one great hand slammed down on the table, the other pointed straight at Frankie. 'You!' he shouted. 'You—' and then an odd thing happened: his thick lips moved and no words came, only a muted rumble like thunder from a distant storm. There was an uncanny resemblance to Hay's stammer. 'Y-y—' The red of his face was deepening, turning the colour of the wine in his glass. 'Y-you!' He found his voice. 'Get out! Get out! Get out!' he shouted. 'Go and wait outside my study; you may cool your heels there in the corridor until I come. I'll see you after p-p-p—' The awful echo of Hay's stammer returned and his eyes started from his head in fury. 'P-p-p—'

Old Blinky gently touched his arm. 'After prayers,' he whispered. 'After prayers, Rufus.'

The Rector swallowed. 'After prayers,' he echoed like a child.

Frankie left the room. Etta watched him.

'Cooley!' the Rector screamed.

Even at this moment, when he must have felt triumphant, Etta still flinched at the sound of his real name. He stood up.

'Cooley, you go and watch him, he's a tricky one, he's cunning. You make sure he stays where he's told till I come.'

Swiftly, Etta followed.

'Eat!' the Rector bellowed at the rest of us. 'Eat!'

Obediently we picked up our forks.

'And you get back to your place. We've had enough of you.' He jabbed a finger at Hay and sat down in his chair. He looked old and tired and I saw Old Blinky lean forward and pat his hand, and I thought of that photograph Frankie had found, where the two of them were boys and there was a white butterfly perched on the back of the future Rector's hand. It didn't make me hate him less, and I saw how Bri Tobin might be right when he talked about getting a black hole inside you and wanting to hurt people and not even knowing you did.

Over at the lectern poor Hay couldn't seem to move. He stood there, shaking all over, until Father Stuckey went across and took the book from his hand and led him back to his place at the juniors' table. And when Hay was settled there, Father Stuckey walked over to the lectern, opened the book and began to read the story to us, right from the beginning.

'At the time when St Francis was living in the city of Gubbio, a large wolf appeared in the neighbourhood, so terrible and so fierce that he not only devoured other animals, but made a prey of men also...'

19.

It was hours before Frankie returned from his summons that night. I'd hurried back, afraid that I'd find his door wide open, Etta and the prefects in there clearing out the room, Frankie expelled already, gone. I pictured a big hand on his shoulder, a push into a car, a swift ride down to the bus stop at Shoreham, another push into the street. Expulsions happened quickly. You never saw them, and the silence, the secrecy, meant you could imagine anything.

When I reached our corridor, Frankie's door was closed. There was no sound from inside.

As I stood there, someone hissed my name. 'Tom!'

Bri Tobin and a group of other boys had gathered at the top of the stairs. 'Is he there?' whispered Bri.

I opened the door and switched on the light. The room was empty and as I looked round, it struck me what a painfully narrow place it was to keep a human being, especially one like Frankie. His dressing gown lay on the bed and I guessed it wouldn't be there if he'd been chucked out and his things all cleared away. Relief swept through me like a tide.

'Not there?' asked Bri.

I shook my head.

'Still with the Rector then.' He frowned.

'It's hours,' said Joey Gertler. 'I wouldn't want to be him.'

'I would,' said Bri, his eyes bright. 'Because he's got guts.'

'He'll get chucked out for sure,' said Dan Yelty.

'So?'

There was a scuffling sound above us. A group of the small kids were hanging over the banister on the landing outside their dorm. Hay was amongst them, his freckles brilliant against the whiteness of his skin. His spiky hair seemed to quiver. The poor kid probably thought that if Frankie got chucked out it would be his fault. 'Will he?' he asked us.

'No one's going to chuck old Frankie out,' Bri Tobin answered him. 'Not unless he wants to go.'

'But will he? Will he go?'

'That's up to him,' Bri said gently, and Hay whispered, 'I don't want him to go,' and a ripple of agreement passed through the small kids, a little lament for what life might be without Frankie. They drifted away into their dormitory and for a few minutes we older ones stood round, talking about Frankie and what might be happening in the Rector's study, then we too drifted back to our rooms. I lay on my bed and waited. Why was Frankie so long with the Rector? I pictured his dressing gown crumpled on the bed—its presence there had suggested the room hadn't been cleared, but what if some prefect, hurrying from the room, had simply dropped it, unnoticed? I closed my eyes and now I thought the dressing gown had exactly that look about it: a dropped look, half on the blanket, the other half trailing to the floor. I tried to remember anything else which might suggest the room hadn't been cleared—notebooks on the desk, a piece of clothing on the back of the chair, but I couldn't, the moment I'd spotted the dressing gown I'd closed the door.

I went to his room, switched on the light and looked round. The desk was bare except for a couple of the rough notebooks he'd used for Bella's love letters. I opened the wardrobe and all his things were still inside, shirts and trousers, the red sweater, an old raincoat I'd never seen before. His underclothes were tumbled in the drawer, his shoes on the floor, an old brown suitcase up on the shelf. As I closed the wardrobe I spotted a piece of paper beneath the chair where he hung his cassock. It was one of the love letters. I picked it up and studied the simple message which seemed to say more than its few plain words, to express the longing which sent him up to the hillside to stare down at the playground of St Brigid's, over and over again. I traced the loops and curves of the word 'love' and wondered what it would be like if the name written there was mine instead of hers. Though I now knew I loved him, I still couldn't imagine how it would be if he loved me instead of Bella. I sensed that whatever happened might come in the same rush of overwhelming joy and desire that his kiss had brought me last night. Beyond that I floundered, unable to see. I didn't know things—back at my old school I often had the feeling that the other boys knew stuff I didn't, had explored a whole continent when my own dreamy ship had barely touched the shore.

I folded the love letter into the pocket of my cassock.

His own pockets would be full of them; he carried them round. What if the Rector asked him to empty out his pockets, like the teachers at my old school used to ask the army camp kids whenever anything valuable went missing? I turned out the light and sat down on the bed. I gathered up the dressing gown and buried my face in it, the folds smelled of the soap they gave us for the shower and something simple and indefinable which made me want to cry. I don't know how long I sat there—once a child whimpered upstairs, once a door opened and closed further down the corridor, perhaps Tim Vesey returning from his lookout window on the landing or someone else coming late to bed. I slipped into a sort of daydream of Frankie living with my parents—it was possible now that this dream might become real. If the Rector threw him out, if his own parents wouldn't have him back, then he could come to us; my parents would have him, I knew. I thought of that room down the hall from mine, how it looked out into the branches of the big apple tree and in summer the air was shadowy and green.

The light snapped on. I looked up and there was Frankie— no one with him, no teacher, no Etta, no posse of prefects come to watch him while he gathered up his things. Just Frankie. 'What're you doing?' he said.

'I came to look for you, to see if you'd come back. To see if your things were still here.'

He nodded. At first glance he looked okay, but when I looked longer I saw that his face seemed slacker, as if the bones had lost their substance and sunk in upon themselves. There was a redness round his eyes. I jumped up from the bed so he could lie down. He didn't want to. 'No, no, you stay there. I'm all right.' He went over to the desk, turned the chair round and sat down on it, his long legs thrust out from his cassock, his boots flexed hard against the floor. He was shaking; the stuff of his trousers was trembling.

'What happened? Are they going to—' I couldn't finish, it didn't matter, he knew what I meant.

'Last chance,' he muttered. 'He gave me one last chance.'

'He did?' I could hardly believe it. 'That—that's good then, isn't it?'

'Yeah.'

'We all thought he'd chuck you out.'

'Well, he didn't. Punishments—the usual sort of stuff: banned from film nights and the bush picnic, essays to write.' He dug the heels of his boots hard against the floor. 'Only this time they're locking me up.'

'Locking you up?' I pictured a dark freezing cellar, damp running down stone walls, and the idea of it must have shown in my face because he smiled faintly and said, 'Oh, not in chains, nothing like that.' The heels dug into the floor again. 'Just— I'm not allowed past the courtyard, except for "supervised activities". No more wandering, no more sneaking up the hill to see if Bella's there, no more watching the sun come up. The lovely world's strictly out of bounds.'

'Ah. Did he know about you going up the hill?'

'He seemed to. I reckon you might have been right about Etta spying on me. When I was in with the Rector, he was listening at the door, I'm sure of it. He wasn't there when I came out, but you know that feeling you get when someone's been in a place the moment before? I could sort of feel him, the air was thick with him, all worked up because I didn't get chucked out. A sort of jangly feel, like you get in your ears when a big storm's coming. Yeah, all spikes and blades and jangles. The Rector—' He stopped and stared down at the floor.

'The Rector?'

He lifted his head and looked right at me. 'First, first he made me wait. You know how he said, "after evening prayers?" Well, it was longer than that, it was hours—standing in the corridor, waiting for him to come, and all the time that little bastard was watching me, sitting on this chair he'd brought from somewhere, reading his prayers. He didn't look at me once but if I'd made the slightest move he'd have been on me like a ferret on a rat. Then the Rector came, and he sent him off, and then he yelled at me, "Get in here!" like I'm a dog, and not anyone's pet either, just some scruffy old stray. He humbled me, Tom. I hate being humbled. I hate it. Remember the Bishop?'

'The Bishop?'

'When we had our interviews, before we came here.

Remember?'

'Oh, yes.'

'Well, did he ask you where everyone slept, in your house?'

'What? Where everyone slept?'

'Yeah. He didn't ask you, did he?'

'No. Why would he ask you a thing like that?'

'Because he thought people like us were all over the place, even if they went to church.'

'What people?'

'Poor people. Oh, my dad had a job all right, but we were still pretty poor— and Dad used to drink a bit. Only a little bit. He used to—' His face took on that stricken look. 'And Mum was a wreck, just about. The bishop would've known about all that, Father Nolan would have told him. To people like them, we were poor, see? All over the place, like rubbish. Sleeping in each other's beds. Doing stuff, you know. That's why he wanted to know where we all slept.'

'He wouldn't think that!'

'Yes, he would. If you're poor, people can think anything about you.'

'Only some people,' I pleaded. 'Only some. Most people are good—you said that, remember? When you were telling me about missing the train, and about how you stayed with the Tooheys, and how Mrs Toohey made you that cake, this high.'

He didn't say anything.

'And those old men on the bench outside the post office, remember? One of them showed you how to make a box kite?'

He rubbed at his eyes. He looked desperately tired. I got up from the bed. 'You get some sleep. I'd better go.' I started walking towards the door and he got up from the chair and followed me, holding out his hand. I didn't know what he wanted, for a dizzying fraction of a second I thought he wanted me, then I noticed he was pointing at my chest and I looked down and saw that I still had his dressing gown, that I was clutching it to me like a kid with some precious toy. 'Oh!' I held it out to him. 'Sorry, I forgot I had it. I—'

'It's all right, it's all right, Tom.' Gently, he took it from me and tossed it onto the bed. He looked into my face. It was the very last time I'd see him. Though of course I didn't know that.

'Thanks,' he said. 'Thanks for being here, Tom.'

I went back to my room and kicked my boots off and lay down on the bed. Frankie got into his bed too, I heard the sounds of it: the boots falling, the rustle of the cassock coming off, the creak of the bed, the shift of his poor body as he turned towards our wall. He must have been so tired.

'Hay's mum and dad will come and get him now, I bet,' he whispered. I'd almost forgotten about poor Hay. Frankie hadn't. 'They'll come and take him home,' he went on. 'And he'll be all right too—they won't think he's a bum, they won't think he's useless just because he didn't want to stay here. He'll be someone one day, Hay Jarrell will. Someone really good, I bet. You could see how they loved him...'

He was less than a metre away from me through that thin partition. When I put my hand against it I could almost feel his warmth. I pictured him lying there, the fingers of one hand smoothing at his blanket, like Hay's mum had stroked her son's back through the stuff of his cassock, up and down and up and down. I couldn't stand it that he thought he had no one to love him like that. I longed to say—the words were there ready on my tongue—'I love you, Frankie.' Only I didn't, he wasn't like me and I didn't know how he'd take it, so I swallowed the words back down.

I didn't ever say them.

20.

If. From now on, everything is *'if'*.

Miri hates it when I go on about *if.* 'Oh don't, Tom!' she pleads, and if I keep on with it she puts her hands over her ears. 'Don't!'

So I don't, not with Miri. I keep *if* to myself.

If I'd told Frankie I loved him that night, would it have made a difference to what happened?

Once I was talking to an old friend about our seminary days. He had entered early, at twelve. 'I was so lonely, so very lonely,' he told me, 'that when this older boy came up to me and whispered, "I love you," I let him make love to me, even though I wasn't gay. It was the word, I think—the simple sound of it, in that place—'

If I'd told Frankie I loved him he might have done this too—made love to me because he desperately needed love that night, and Bella was a daydream, and he liked me even though he wasn't gay. He came from a more pragmatic, less sheltered world than I; he'd have given love to me if he thought I wanted it.

He was always a kind boy. And then he wouldn't have gone out that night.

I never told him because I was too afraid. I fell asleep and when I woke, perhaps only twenty minutes later, I could tell that he'd gone.

I didn't go after him, I guessed he might want to be by himself on this last night before his confinement to the courtyard was known and enforced—he'd want to be out in the great spaces of the headland, walking off his humiliation at the hands of the Rector, wandering his lovely, lovely world. Only then I began to think of Etta, of his anger and frustration that Frankie had escaped expulsion again—those blades and spikes and jangles that Frankie had sensed in the corridor outside the Rector's study. *Blades and spikes and jangles*: the words reminded me how right at the beginning I'd dreaded that if I spoke Etta's name to Frankie it would set off some dreadful mechanism which could never be stopped in time. Now it seemed I'd been right. And Etta *knew* Frankie, he'd most certainly guess that he'd go out wandering tonight; he'd go after him.

If. If I'd gone straight away I might have reached Frankie in time, while he was still on the hillside, before he'd gone, as he must have done, to wait for the sunrise from the ledge above the sea.

If, as I hurried along the path beside the teachers' garden, that same brilliant sickle moon hadn't swept out from behind a cloud and picked out the tap, the one Frankie had drunk from the evening Father James had called me to his study. It glinted like a malicious secret against the dark bushes and I stopped—I stopped because a memory came sweeping over me, a great gritty wave that squeezed the breath right from my chest. I saw Frankie stooping over that tap, his blond hair and red sweater luminous in that fading light, and then, when he'd gone, Etta coming out from his hiding place and putting his lips where Frankie's sweet lips had been. I saw his rapturous face, his finger pressed to his lips to seal in the taste of Frankie.

I realised, finally. Etta was in love with Frankie: everything was as simple as that. It had been simple all along. The watching, the spying, that invisible line I'd sensed drawn between them down in Shoreham: that was love, Etta's love, burning itself through the air. Everything inside me seemed to writhe, each muscle and organ, each nerve, each tiny cell. That Etta could feel as I did! It horrified me—that he might lie awake and think about Frankie, that he might long to touch that buttery golden hair, to take Frankie's hand and kiss those long brown fingers, one by one—

Give me a thousand kisses, then a hundred,
Then another thousand ...

Plunging from the path I pushed my way into the bushes and found the kind of dark, secret refuge where a child might hide. And there I crouched, clutching at a handful of some spicy smelling plant, crushing its leaves in my hot fingers. Sometimes at night I'd press my burning forehead up against the cold surface of the wall between us as if it was the warm roundness of Frankie's shoulder that I leaned into, the smoothness of his skin I kissed. The thought that Etta might also do something like that was like poison rushing through my blood. He couldn't! He couldn't!

And suddenly I knew he couldn't. At least, I thought I knew. I thought: if Etta loved Frankie like I did, then he would never want him sent away, he would want to be near him forever. I didn't see the rest of it. It never occurred to me that Etta might see his love for Frankie as depraved and vile and dangerous, a demon to be cast out. I didn't understand, not for a long, long time.

I crept out of my refuge and made my way towards the hillside.

If. If I'd gone a little earlier, instead of continuing to sit there in a kind of trance, paralysed, still crushing those small soft leaves in my hand—because of course, when I reached the top of the hill, Frankie wasn't there. He had been, I could see that, the sickle moon showed me a small scattering of his love letters on the ground. Not many, no more than a handful, and I guessed he'd taken them from his pockets for comfort, 'to look at', and then, for some reason, simply let them fall. I snatched them up and crammed them into my pockets. Then I began calling him; distraught as I was, I didn't care who heard. There was a strange tumbling feeling inside my skull, as if everything in there was turning, falling, rearranging itself.

'Frankie!' I called. 'Frankie!'—stumbling towards the gap in the wall, peering down at St Brigid's. Tonight the outside light had been switched on, illuminating the entry and a big spiky holly bush beside the porch. Outside the gates a single street lamp shone on the empty road. There was a wind now, a tricky giddy little wind, and I watched it chase a small piece of paper playfully down the road, lifting it a little, dropping it down again. It was a neat piece of paper, perfectly square, and I knew immediately it was one of Frankie's love letters. My eyes darted back to the holly bush beside the porch, I'd half registered something white caught on the thorny leaves. Now I saw it was another love letter, held fast. When the wind blew it waved and fluttered like a small white hand.

For a moment I imagined Frankie climbing over those tall gates, 'posting' the letter on the thorny branch for Bella to find. I dismissed the idea at once. There was a strain of sound common sense in Frankie; he'd know Bella wouldn't be the one to find the letter, he'd know he'd get her into trouble. The wind had taken it there. I heard footsteps, Frankie coming up the hill behind me. Still peering at the letter, trying to work out how we could get in to St Brigid's and retrieve it, I called back over my shoulder, 'There's one of your love letters down there, it's stuck in this bush next to the door. They'll find it.'

He didn't answer. I turned round and there was Etta.

He looked different. That was the only thing I registered in that first moment of utter frozen shock: how he looked different. I didn't take in properly what that difference was, except that he looked *wrong*. It was only later I worked out that it lay in an air of disarray: he had always been so immaculate, now his normally shiny boots were caked with grey muddy sand and there were smears of it along the hem of his cassock. The cassock itself was crumpled and damp-looking, and there was a button missing from the top, the second one down. It had been torn off, you could see the small clean rip in the fabric where it had been. And he was holding another of Frankie's letters in his hand. Without speaking, he stepped forward to the gap in the wall and looked down at the school, and I had no doubt he saw the white scrap of paper fluttering from the holly tree and knew at once what it was, because a little hiss escaped his lips, though he still said nothing to me.

From the road below I heard the sound of a car and Etta must have heard it too, though he gave no sign of it. A taxi was coming towards St Brigid's. It stopped outside the gates and after a minute a teacher got out from the passenger side and stood on the footpath, searching in the pocket of her habit for a key. The taxi drove off and she unlocked the gates and went inside, closing them behind her. She walked up the path to the porch and knocked on the door. She didn't notice the piece of white paper in the bush beside her until a little gust of wind set it fluttering, and then she picked it from the bush like you'd pick a flower. She saw the writing and bent her head to read.

The front door was opened by the grey-haired woman Frankie and I had seen through the lighted window the night before. The teacher held the note out to her; she glanced at it, said something, and then they both turned and looked up towards St Finbar's, as if they knew it had come from there.

I thought of the brief message on the note: *Bella, my beautiful, beautiful Bella, I love you—Frankie Maguire.*

'They'll be on the phone to the Rector first thing in the morning,' murmured Etta.

I turned towards him. His deep-set eyes seemed larger, closer to the surface; they had a strange, shocked expression. I saw that he hadn't really been speaking to me, he seemed barely to notice me—he was talking to himself. 'He'd have been out before lunchtime anyway,' he went on in that same strange sleepwalker's voice. 'He'd have been gone. *Gone.* I needn't have done anything. I needn't have.' The reedy voice tailed away and I heard a small dry rasping sound; his tiny hands were clutched round his forearms, wringing and writhing, the movements a person might make washing grease off his arms after some messy little job. He saw me watching and his hands fell slowly to his sides.

I couldn't understand him. I couldn't understand why he was talking in the past tense, as if Frankie had already gone from St Finbar's. I couldn't understand why he wanted Frankie gone, anyway. Not if he loved him.

I said so.

'I don't know why you want him sent away.'

He didn't reply, though I knew he'd heard me because his face twitched and his throat moved slightly as if he was trying to swallow something that wouldn't go down. I was on the verge of tears myself, and what I said next was really about my loss as much as his. 'If he gets chucked out you'll never see him again.'

He screamed at me. The sound was so shocking, so raw and terrible, that it took me a moment to work out his words. 'Don't *say* that! I don't *want* to see him! Why do you think I want to see him? I don't! I *don't*!' Then he swung away from me and rushed off down the hill.

21.

'You were so lucky with your parents,' Miri said to me one time. 'So lucky with Uncle David and Aunty Clare.'

She was right, of course. In a time when for most people homosexuality was seen as either farcical or morally degraded, I grew up thinking there was nothing really wrong with being gay. I knew there were many who didn't share my parents' views—the only time I ever saw my father really angry was the weekend when the windows of Joseph and Denny's bookshop were smashed, and *Perverts, Out!* scrawled in thick red paint across the doors. I knew that being gay was going to be hard but I also believed what my parents had taught me, that we were people who could also love, and it was the love that counted.

Etta would have grown up differently. I only have to picture his parents: the tall ascetic man and the pale woman who came to visit him at St Finbar's on that freezing winter's day, and I know that in his family homosexuality would never have been mentioned, simply because it was unmentionable. His parents would have agreed with St Thomas Aquinas when he wrote that homosexuality was 'a special kind of deformity'.

Etta himself would have agreed. The attraction he felt for Frankie would have seemed vile to him, like the workings of an evil spirit inside his body. 'He hates himself,' Frankie had said with his sure instinct, and of course he was right. Etta would hate himself and he would fear any beautiful boy for whom he felt that stirring, which in other people would have been the beginnings of love. 'Etta gets these *downs* on people,' John Rushall had told me, 'and then he wants to get them out, away from here.' Etta's ambitions meant that he had to be seen to be pure.

'Imagine that!' Miri said to me. 'Imagine thinking you were deformed inside.' I remember she shivered, and added with one of those sidelong glances, 'You'd do anything to hide it. *Anything*.'

Of course, I understood none of this that night I met Etta on the hillside. None of it. I went back to the seminary expecting to find Frankie in his room, and when he wasn't there, I simply thought he was still wandering his lovely, lovely world. I would leave him in peace on this last night of freedom. I thought he was safe. I knew Etta was back, when I'd passed the prefects' rooms I'd seen the sliver of light shining from beneath his blind. I wasn't thinking properly; already the cloudiness was forming at the bottom of my mind. I went to Frankie's room and sat down at his desk, took a few sheets of paper from the notebooks he'd used for his love letters and wrote out my parents' address for him, and a note he could give to them. 'Just in case,' I told myself. In case Etta was right and the nuns from St Brigid's rang in the morning, and Frankie was 'out by lunchtime'. Would he be? I didn't know, I felt I didn't know anything, and perhaps after all Etta didn't know anything either. After all, the nuns hadn't told on Frankie that long-ago day when he'd walked across the road to Bella down in Shoreham. My head ached. I reached for another sheet of paper and wrote a note for Frankie: *If you ever need to, you can come and live with us*—I scribbled out the 'us' and put 'them', and then I changed my mind and crossed out 'them' and put 'us' again, and then I sat there looking at the small word for a long time, wondering whether it would put him off or not. Finally I left it there, folded the notes and went to the wardrobe, where I slipped them into the pockets of his spare trousers, the ones he would most likely wear if he had to leave.

As I came out of his room one of the small kids upstairs began to cry. It sounded louder out there in the corridor, and it went on and on, the same old aching sound. Back in sixth class, Sister Honoria had once given us a composition: 'What would Jesus think if he came to our school?' Now, my ears full of that desolate crying, I wondered what Jesus would think if he came to St Finbar's and I had a pretty good idea it would be like the story of the money changers in the temple: Jesus would rage through St Finbar's, knocking over the long tables in the refectory, tearing open the big steel fridges and the locked cupboards in the kitchen, spilling their contents on the floor, barging into the Rector's study and strewing his papers round—

Upstairs the little kid was still crying and suddenly another voice, young like his, but newly tough and merciless, growled out savagely, 'Shut up!' The little kid went silent at once and I ran to the landing and shouted up the stairs, 'You shut up! *You* shut up!' My voice echoed along the corridor, all the kids on our floor would have heard it, just like they'd have heard the little kid crying and the savage one telling him to shut up, silencing him. No one came. No one did anything. It was like Frankie said that time on the hill when I told him about Bri Tobin's outburst down at the handball courts: 'They're scared.' And Bri was right when he'd said, 'You feel like you're getting this hard place, this little black hole inside you and some day you might even want to hurt people and—and you won't even know you do.'

And perhaps I was getting like that because all at once the only thing I wanted was to go and look at the sea—not those big waves that came crashing up against the cliffs on stormy nights. I wanted the gentle sea Frankie and I had watched together that afternoon down in Shoreham. I wanted that calm, unending movement that he'd loved so much, that reminds you of the word 'forever' and brings a kind of peace.

I went into my room and took my coat from the wardrobe— like Hay Jarrell's mum, my own mother had bought it a size too large in the hopes that I would grow. It almost covered my cassock and down in Shoreham no one would recognise me as a boy from St Finbar's.

Out in the courtyard the slit of light was still shining beneath Etta's blind. A sudden urgent curiosity drew me to that window, it felt like need. I *had* to see Etta on his own, in the place where he felt hidden, safe. I crossed the courtyard towards that narrow beam, stooped down and put my eye to the gap between the sill and the blind. I don't know quite what I expected to see, and my heart beat so loudly I thought he might hear it through the glass.

He was sitting cross-legged in the middle of the floor, wearing a purple dressing gown trimmed with gold braid. At first I thought something terrible had happened to his hands, they were blood red, the colour of fresh raw meat—then I realised he was wearing rubber gloves, the kind my mother used for cleaning. There was a sheet of newspaper on his lap, and another spread on the floor in front of him, a soft yellow cloth lay on it, and a tin of polish and a boot. The second boot was in his hands. He was cleaning it with a small black brush, carefully removing the sticky grey sand which caked its sole and heel. His cleaning would be meticulous, there wouldn't be a trace of that grey stuff left when he'd finished; the boot already sitting on the newspaper shone like new. His cassock hung on the knob of the wardrobe door, wiped clean, the small rent mended, a new button sewn on. He would have such things, I thought contemptuously, brushes and polish, soft cloth, needle and thread and new buttons; his mother would have packed them for him because he had to look perfect, all the time.

Absorbed in his task, he had no idea that I was watching him. He appeared oddly content, composed, like a person who has been frightened but now has a happy idea. 'Once every grain of this sand is removed,' he might have been thinking, 'then everything is going to be all right for me.' His lips were moving and somehow I knew it wasn't a prayer he was saying, like you might expect from the head prefect of St Finbar's in the early hours of the morning. No, Etta was singing to himself, I could tell from the almost jaunty way he swung his head. I wondered what the song was. The whole scene: the lighted room, the night outside, Etta's cross-legged posture, his smallness, the boots, was like a scene from the story of the shoemaker and the elves. And I thought of that other story, *Rumpelstiltskin*, and wondered what he'd do if I suddenly tapped on the window and called out his true name, *Brian Cooley*! Would he have torn himself in two?

I don't know, because I didn't call his name. Instead, I hurried away. I needed my gentle sea.

*

It was almost light when I got down to Shoreham. I passed a milkman with his horse and cart in the first streets of the town. He was a big rangy man with a sunburned face and a mop of dark blond hair, the sort of man Frankie might be when he was middle-aged. 'Early start, eh?' he said, and I felt a little thrill of happiness as if the ordinary world was folding me into it again. As I passed the bus stop I thought how I could even go home. I had money—despite my protests my mother had insisted on sewing two five-pound notes into the hem of my overcoat. 'Just in case,' she'd said. Everything depended on what happened to

Frankie: as long as he stayed, I would stay. If they expelled him then I would go too.

I walked towards the beach along a street of small homely shops which were exactly like the ones in the side streets of the suburb where my parents lived, and in all the side streets of all the suburbs like it: a small grocery, a haberdashery with a bright display of knitting wools in the window, a milk bar where the lady who was folding back the shutters called out to me, 'Beautiful morning, isn't it, love? Looks like it's going to be a beautiful day!'

It did look like that. The wind had dropped and the sky was clear except for a flock of small white fluffy clouds floating along the horizon. When I reached the beach I took off my boots and the sand felt silky beneath my feet, a pale whitish gold in the early light. Further down it was damp and firm, the colour of rich toffee, nothing like that coarse grey stuff that had been on Etta's boots and cassock. The thought of that stuff made me feel sick. I didn't want to think about where it had come from, I hummed to myself to push it away. *Hushabye, don't you cry*— As I reached the water's edge the sun was beginning its rising, a round edge of rosy gold above the horizon. The little clouds turned pink and then the sea turned pink, the whole wide swell of it, right up to the small lacy waves running over my feet, so that it looked like a great rose-coloured quilt flung down upon the sand. I was flooded with joy, the very same joy I'd seen so often on Frankie's face when he saw something beautiful in his lovely, lovely world.

'Oh, look!' I whispered, 'look!' and for a moment I actually thought he was there. I felt him standing right beside me, I felt his warmth and heard his long sigh of pure happiness, 'Ah-ah.' I turned to smile at him. He wasn't there, the sigh was only the sound of the sea turning and folding itself on the sand.

Across the Esplanade a clock chimed six slow strokes. Up at St Finbar's they'd be getting up, grabbing their boots and cassocks, heading for the showers. Frankie would be back by now. I turned from the rosy sea and hurried up the sand and past the little shops and into the road that led towards St Finbar's. It was early morning now; the gates of St Brigid's stood open and out in the garden a group of girls in lumpy gym tunics were doing calisthenics with one of the teachers. I saw Bella with the rest of them, her thick dark hair tumbling from its ribbon again. As I passed she stood still and stared at me and then the other girls stared and the teacher swung round and for a moment I thought they might recognise me from that long-ago day when Bella had smiled at Frankie.

But I don't think they did recognise me. In my long overcoat I was only an ordinary, not very handsome boy walking along the road. The teacher made a swift little chopping motion with one hand and the girls' glances swerved away from me and they went on with their exercises. As I hurried on I heard one of them laugh, and I'm sure it was Bella—it was a beautiful laugh, warm and soft as those rosy little waves down on the beach, no trace of meanness or mockery in it—simply the sound of the lovely, lovely world.

22.

Back at the seminary, I found Frankie still hadn't returned. Nothing had been touched in his room, his clothes and bag were still in the wardrobe, my notes, 'just in case', still tucked into the pocket of his spare trousers. Only—he wasn't in chapel that morning and his place was empty all day at mealtimes and in the classes we shared. I saw people glance at that space and a queer little ripple of fear was in the air, the ripple that spread through all of us whenever a student who'd been in his place, every day, suddenly wasn't there anymore. Frankie didn't come back that day, or that night, or the next day or the next night— or any night or any day. He didn't come back at all.

*

For once we were told; at least we were told that Frankie hadn't been expelled. This might have been because the police came—not right away, not that day or the next. They came a week or so after Frankie had disappeared. I suppose by that time the Rector must have contacted the Maguires and learned that he hadn't come home. The single black police car was parked discreetly at the far end of the courtyard, near that vine-covered veranda where I'd once asked John Rushall why Etta hadn't reported Frankie for breaking St Finbar's rules.

I hadn't seen Etta since the night on the hillside. There was a story going round that he'd caught pneumonia and been taken to hospital in the city and then to his home to convalesce. The two policemen were with the Rector for less than an hour, and after that they drove away. There was no search, none of us were questioned.

In those early days I found I wasn't the only student who knew about Frankie's wanderings. Almost everyone in our year had noticed how he used to slip away to the top of the hill above St Brigid's, there were even rumours that he'd had a girlfriend down there. Hay's parents had come for him, exactly as Frankie had said, so it was one of the other little kids who came up to me in the courtyard and asked if it was true that Frankie had run off to get married. I told him no, and he shoved his hands in his pockets and made a long sound of disappointment, 'Awweerrr—' I suppose they thought running off to get married was more romantic than simply running away.

Tim Vesey knew about the ledge on the cliff; he'd even been there. 'Spooky, isn't it?' he said. 'Sort of,' I answered. I didn't want to think of that place.

Tim stood there quietly in front of me, shifting his weight from foot to foot and I knew he was going to ask me something else and I felt afraid of what it might be. Finally he came out with it. 'Do you think he could have—you know, um—' His face coloured slightly, his eyes avoided mine, and I knew he meant could Frankie have gone to that ledge and jumped off it. 'No,' I said firmly, because of that one thing I was completely sure. 'No, he never would,' and Tim beamed at me. 'That's what I think! He *never* would! He wasn't that kind of person! He was—he just liked everything in the world! Don't you think?'

'Yes.'

'He left, that's all! And no wonder!' Tim walked off quite jauntily.

Most people believed this: that after the scene in the refectory and his long interview with the Rector, Frankie had simply left of his own accord. It seemed the logical explanation: the police had found nothing, his body was never washed up on the rocks or surrounding beaches in the weeks that followed. People did run away, and sometimes, like Frankie, they left no note and told no one, not even their best friends. And if they came from very pious families like Frankie's, they might not go home for a very long time, out of fear and shame. They might find a new life up north or in one of the big cities and start their lives all over again. You could see why everyone believed he'd run off, sometimes even I was on the verge of believing it, only then I'd remember the look on his face that time he'd said, 'I'd never leave!'—that shocked amazement, the way his eyes had seemed to become darker, that brilliant indigo swallowed by a blackness that was fierce and bright. No, I knew he wouldn't leave.

Only, if he hadn't left, where was he? The question troubled me; I didn't want to ask it, not even of myself, and as the days passed a deep confusion settled over my mind. At times I could barely remember the events of that night; at others stark images would rear up out of nowhere: the moon glinting on the tap in the teachers' garden, grey sand on a crumpled cassock with a button torn away, a ledge of pitted rock, a great sea merging into endless sky. One afternoon, a few weeks after his disappearance, I slipped off from sport and made my way up the hill and along the wall until I came to the sandy track through blackberries and lantana. I was wild with some kind of urgency. I ran, barely registering the tough winter brambles catching at my sweater, tearing at my legs and arms. I had to *see* that place again. When I burst from the track onto the ledge I gasped, I'd forgotten how the sea and sky seemed to leap out at you. I dropped to my hands and knees. I hardly knew what I was doing; it seemed I was looking for something though I didn't know what it was. It was *something*, some tiny sign, some indication that Frankie had been there that night. Was that it? Was that what I wanted to find? Evidence? Of what? I peered into every crack and hollow, I plunged my hands into the murky water of the small pools, raking my fingertips along the slimy rock, searching. I found nothing. Back in my room that night, for the very first time I cried and cried.

The next afternoon I slipped away again. This time I went to the gap in the wall where Frankie used to look down into the garden of St Brigid's. I chose the middle of the afternoon when the girls had their break because I wanted to see if Bella was there. I wanted to rid myself of an idea that would take hold of me in the middle of the night: that after all there'd been more to Frankie's love than daydreams, that he'd had secrets he'd never told me, that he and Bella had got to know each other, that they met secretly. And if they had then he'd have contacted her, sent her a letter—the idea was all the stronger and more painful because he'd left no message for me. In the dark early hours of the morning this story would reach a kind of crescendo inside my head: perhaps by now she too had run away. Perhaps they were together.

But when I looked down on that soft green garden with its big trees and gravel paths, Bella was there, sitting on a bench in a sunny corner, laughing with her friend. There was no change in her, nothing of that particular gravity I had come to associate with love. She looked exactly the same. I kept on going back. She could still get a letter, and I thought I'd be able to tell if she did, that then there'd be some sign. For a while there was nothing, until one afternoon—spring was coming and I remember it was a cold blowy day with bursts of sunshine and sudden brief showers, and Bella and her friend had got up from their bench and run laughing towards the shelter of the porch—and suddenly I understood that there really *was* nothing, nothing on Bella's side, anyway. One day down in Shoreham she'd smiled at a boy from the seminary and he'd walked halfway across the road towards her and then a teacher had called out and they'd all moved on—it was ages ago, she probably didn't even remember now. 'Frankie? Who's he?' she'd have wondered if I'd met her in the street and asked if she'd heard from him.

I'd been jealous of Bella receiving a letter, yet now in the middle of the night I'd think it would be better if she had. Then I'd ask myself, 'Better than what?'

Better than silence, better than not knowing anything, better than—and at this point a cloud would roll over my mind and hide the thoughts inside it. And then those images would come rearing up: the glinting tap, the sandy hem of Etta's cassock, the grey ledge above the sea. I pushed them away. I was afraid of them. I kept on watching Bella, sneaking away from sport almost every day. And then one afternoon John Rushall came up to me and we sat down on the grass to talk. Like almost everyone, John believed Frankie had run away.

'But he left all his stuff,' I said. How feeble it sounded, like a child. 'All his clothes, and his shoes, and his bag, and—' I was about to say 'dressing gown' and stopped myself just in time. Before they'd cleared Frankie's room I'd taken that dressing gown and hidden it amongst my own things. At night I slept with it pressed against my chest.

'Look, Tom, sometimes it happens like that. You just—go. You're out walking, somewhere you shouldn't be, most likely, and all of a sudden everything wells up in you, all of it: you just go. It's like you can't bear to go back to your room, or anywhere in that building, even to get your things, you leave in whatever you're standing up in—*whoosh!* That's it!'

He sounded like he might have done it, one time. And he'd come back. Somehow I knew Frankie wouldn't. He wouldn't come back.

Etta had returned from his convalescence. He looked the same as ever, small, white-skinned and quiet, with his big domed head and neat little creature's paws. Sometimes I thought I'd dreamed my meeting with him on the hillside that night, dreamed the messed-up cassock and the strange things he'd said and that terrible screaming cry, like something you trod on in the dark. Dreamed that vision of him in his room cleaning the grey sand from his boots. Perhaps I had. Sometimes I think I dreamed the whole of St Finbar's. Only Frankie seems real.

'He'll be okay,' John said to me that afternoon. 'A great kid like that, wherever he goes he'll be okay.' I thought of Frankie that time he'd missed the train and got stranded in a country town with no money. He'd been okay then, strangers had looked after him, loved him even. John was right—wherever Frankie was, he'd be okay. There was nothing I could do. From then on I used to repeat that to myself at night: 'There's nothing I can do.'

John patted me on the shoulder. He said, 'Don't worry, eh? Just get on with it. Take my word, it might be a while, but you'll hear from him one day.'

I did take his word. I settled down. I learned to live with that patch of cloudiness always at the bottom of my mind.

One day—it was after a night when the images had appeared again— I went back to the ledge and searched those cracks and hollows again, scraped my fingers along the bottoms of the pools. Sometimes you don't find the thing you're looking for the very first time. I didn't find it the second time, either.

23.

I stayed on at St Finbar's and became a priest.

I did it for love, though not the love of God, which I still couldn't understand. I could barely imagine that confident boy who'd believed he could feel God's hand stretched protectively above his head—could that really have been me? It was the love of Frankie that kept me there. St Finbar's was the place where I'd known him, and so many little things kept him close to me: a shaft of sunlight through a high window in the chapel, a flag flapping from the tower, even the portrait of the old Archbishop in the hallway, which I could never pass without hearing Frankie's bright voice exclaiming, *Look! I'm hugging the Archbishop, see! Look, I'm kissing him now!* Kissing him.

There was another reason why I stayed. I've kept it to myself, I've told no one, not even Miri, though sometimes I suspect she knows. I don't even like to write it down here, and I won't, not yet.

*

My mind back in those days resembled the strata of some ancient rockface: at the very bottom there was that cloudiness, a muddy darkness of which I was afraid, above that reared those sudden images, the glinting tap, the muddy hem, the ledge. And above them were the wide plain spaces of everyday for which I felt grateful: prayers and classes and meals in the refectory, laughing boys in the line for the handball courts, for a few weeks speculating on what Frankie might be getting up to out there in the world, and John Rushall's cheerful voice assuring me, 'You'll hear from him one day.'

I kept my hope of that. Of hearing from him. On my first posting to a small town in South Australia, my hand would tremble as I opened the lid of the dented old letterbox beside the front gate. Half a century on, it still trembles when I go to get the post. Even here, in my old house in Currawong, when the phone rings there'll be a small flicker of anticipation that after all John Rushall might have been right and the caller will be Frankie at long last. And always there's that little jump inside me when my computer, unknown in our time, throws up the message *Receiving Mail*. Frankie would be almost seventy now, like me, but why not? Isn't it at our age that you start thinking of old friends? Old places? Home?

I looked for him, of course. There was that first, long-delayed trip to Currawong, but every place I went I kept my eyes open; it was possible I could simply run into him, miraculously. Such things happen. 'With God, all things are possible,' the angel told the Virgin Mary. I'm never sure I believe in God: some days I do, some days I don't—it was Frankie who believed every single day. And once, just once, I thought I'd found him. I'd been celebrating the wedding of a former student in the church at Myall, that same small seaside town where I'd seen those beautiful mysterious patches of indigo floating on the sea, and caught my first glimpse of St Finbar's up there on the hill. After the reception I went down to the beach, took off my shoes and walked across the rocks to the sea-baths where my parents and I had spread our towels to sunbathe on that long-ago beautiful day. Now it was another beautiful day and those indigo patches still floated on the water and to see them gave me that feeling of richness, they made my heart turn over. Across the water St Finbar's stood bravely on its headland, sharply edged against the cloudless sky. There was no flag flying that day, and St Finbar's itself would have only a few more years as a seminary before the building and its grounds were sold and refurbished as a conference centre for business executives. Already on the road beneath it, the place where Frankie had first seen Bella, there were huge new houses and towering apartment blocks. Even sleepy Myall had its changes; as I made my way back along the rocks to the beach my eye was caught by the new Surf Life Saving Club built on the foreshore where the old changing sheds used to be. It was a modern building, faintly Spanish, its white stuccoed brick flushed by the setting sun. There was something eerily familiar about its facade: the arcade with its rounded arches, the parapet along the roof, that small squat turret that looked a little like a belfry.

From where I was standing, halfway back along the rocks, St Finbar's was still visible. I glanced from that old building on the cliff to the new one on the sand and there wasn't a doubt in my mind that the Myall Surf Life Saving Club—its wooden decks scattered with umbrella'd tables and people in summer clothes, their laughter spilling out across the water—had been built as a small earthly replica of St Finbar's. The sturdy little belfry was like a mocking hand raised in salute to its heavenly cousin up there on the hill.

I thought: Frankie.

Over the years, whenever I'd wondered about him out there somewhere in the world, I'd been unable to imagine his occupation. Teacher? Social worker? Engineer? Nothing seemed to fit him. Ordinary occupations seemed too tame. I pictured him wandering from place to place like some itinerant monk of the Middle Ages, talking to people, gathering a little band of faithful followers. Once I asked Miri what she thought he might have become. She looked at me sideways, sadly. 'He had charm,' she said. 'He had charisma. He could have been anything.'

Anything. On the beach at Myall that sunny afternoon, I thought, 'He could have been an architect.'

I ran those last metres from the rocks, stumbling up the sand. Red-faced, out of breath, filled with a kind of hopeless unbelievable joy, I reached the building and circled it, searching for the plaque which would show me his name.

It was easy enough to find, a simple pewter-coloured

metal square set into the wall beside the big glass doors. My fingers met its cool surface with a tender reverence, touched the date (he would have been fifty-six that year), the names of dignitaries and benefactors—and last of all, the architect. It wasn't Frankie. The name was Hayden Jarrell. Hay! I saw his small freckled face, the spiky, straw-coloured hair, and I heard Frankie's voice saying clearly through our wall that last night, 'He'll be *someone*, some day.' And he was: a whole caravan of letters followed Hay's name. I saw Frankie in that dark little courtyard behind the St Finbar's kitchen handing out the precious fruit to Hay and the other kids, and the oranges glowed like small globes of purest light in that murky gloom. And all at once I started to laugh, I don't know why. *Hope deferred makes the heart sick,* perhaps. I laughed so hard, so hopelessly, that I sank down to my knees. Those were still the days when priests wore clerical suits and the people on the deck beneath those big striped umbrellas looked down in amazement, and a little kid called out, 'What's wrong with that man?'

24.

Miri is here. She comes to visit me at Currawong several times a year, driving her beat-up Range Rover over the dusty pot-holed roads. When I hear the roar of its engine in the street I go out to the gate to meet her. The Rover's door will open and she'll emerge, slowly—and then stand for a long moment, gazing at me, like she used to do when we were children and the holiday was over and she was going back home again, standing at the top of the Fokker Friendship's steps, waving and waving until the hostess caught hold of her and whisked her out of sight. 'Tom!' she'll say at last, and when I hear her voice I get that same feeling of richness I had from those deep blue patches floating on the sea. Indigo. She walks with a cane now, leaning heavily to one side, yet in some of her movements—the toss of her head, the wave of a hand, I can still make out the springing, dancing essence of the girl she used to be.

She didn't approve of me taking this retirement post so I could live in Frankie's old home town. She calls me a romantic, she scolds me, she tells me to 'get a life'.

'Love is a fire no waters avail to quench, no floods to drown,' I quoted once when she was scolding, and I saw her face soften at the beautiful words before she shook her head. 'You need to get out more,' she said. Old as I am, she still wants me to *get this life*, which means: she wants me to find someone. 'Someone *real*', as she puts it (though Frankie is real to me). Somebody who will love me like Chris loved her and she loved Chris, like my mother and father loved each other, or Joseph and Den.

Give me a thousand kisses, then a hundred,
Then another thousand, then a second hundred

'There must be some nice men in there,' she says. By 'in there' she means the priesthood. Vows of celibacy don't mean much to Miri, she thinks they're bad for us. 'Or you could find someone outside. You're quite good-looking for your age.' She waves a wrinkled hand, '*Out* there, Tom. Any*where*—' the last syllable is like a sigh, she knows I won't leave Currawong.

'I'll never find anyone like Frankie.'

'Oh, *Tom*.'

I can see what she's thinking. It's there in her face, like it always is. Waste: she thinks my love has been a waste. I'm not angry with her; I understand how she could think this way. And it is true that I was the one who did all the loving. Yet does that matter? 'Isn't it enough that there *is* love?' I ask her. 'That it exists. That a person *can* love, no matter if there's only one person in the equation? My father used to say that being able to love another person was the most important thing.'

'Oh, Tom, Tom—' and she takes my hand and holds it between both of hers and I want to give her something, I want to give her *reasons*.

And so I tell her suddenly that other reason why I stayed on at St Finbar's and became a priest. The one I've kept secret, never telling anyone. 'It was that time we were up on the hillside and he was so unhappy, that time he said, "They may as well cut our balls off!" and I said, "You could always leave." He was so shocked, Miri, so—amazed. He said, "I'll never leave!" and there was this look on his face, Miri, like a kind of rapture—I know he meant it. I know he wanted to stay, more than anything on earth. He'd made that promise, see? And then—' my voice falters, she's staring so hard at me, 'and then after all, he—he couldn't stay. So I took it on for him, I kept the promise for him. I stayed instead of him.'

I stop. My heart is pounding in my chest at the thought of what she's going to say. The reply I expect is the sensible one, because Miri's always sensible and she has no truck with my romantic notions. So I don't know why my heart is pounding, since I know just what she's going to reply—it will be along these lines: 'But Tom, he *did* leave. He ran away. He changed his mind, he didn't care about that promise anymore. He wouldn't have wanted you to live a life he'd decided he no longer wanted—to go and live it for *him*. To waste your life for him! Of course he wouldn't!'

Only—she doesn't say it. She doesn't say anything. Instead

her eyes slide away from mine as if she's embarrassed, like your eyes might slide away from a dying friend who keeps on saying he's well. My heart stops pounding then; it begins to beat steadily and evenly though I don't feel steady and even; it's like it's trying to fool someone, pretending.

She knows. I feel terrified. 'I'll go make us a cuppa,' I say, backing away from her into the kitchen.

My hands are shaking as I fill the jug and set a fan of her favourite biscuits out on a plate. I think, *she knows,* and I wonder how long she has known, how long she has put up with my pretending, my dearest Miri. In the room next door I hear the TV go on, the sound muffled because I've closed the kitchen door. When I take the tray in, Miri is sitting very still with her eyes fixed on the screen.

Etta is there.

You do see him on the screen from time to time. He's gone far in the church, though not as far as we boys at St Finbar's expected him to go. For certain church matters they use him as spokesman—he's quite unflappable, everyone says so, there's never a trace of flush on those pallid cheeks, never the faintest indication of humour, of rage or shame. His voice still holds a trace of the reediness of the fifteen-year-old, but what he says is always calm and rational. However close his opponents may come, Etta is never roused. The sign of a true psychopath, I think.

'It's him,' says Miri, turning.

'I know,' I say, calm as a psychopath myself, arranging the

cups and saucers carefully on the table.

'Want me to change the channel?'

'No, it's okay.' When he comes on and I'm alone I turn him off at once. Now Miri is here, now I know she's guessed my secret, I go on watching. I don't sit down. I stand.

His soutane is immaculate, his shoes shine. There are times when I think I must have imagined him up there on the hillside the night that Frankie disappeared: that air of dishevelment, the damp hair and crumpled cassock, its hem smeared with greyish sand, that little rent where the second button used to be. Imagined that strange hasty way in which he spoke, the things he said, that last terrible scream, as if he were undone. Yes, that's it. Undone. He was undone, because he—

Perhaps I dreamed it, like the time I dreamed St Thomas Aquinas was sitting on my bed. I could have. I had lots of dreams back then. Except there's those little white paws, clasping and unclasping, right here, right now, washing and wringing on my television screen, still struggling to get clean. I can almost hear the raspy whispery sound of that parched tormented skin.

'Oh, look,' whispers Miri. 'Look what he's doing with his hands. Like Lady Macbeth.' I say nothing, and she turns round in her chair. 'Are you all right, Tom?'

Because I'm halfway across the room already, walking backwards towards the doorway. I hold out my hands to her, palms upward, as if to push her concern away. 'Fine, fine,' I say. 'Need a breath of fresh air, that's all. Out on the veranda.

In your beautiful glider.'

'I should have switched the channel.'

'No, no, that's all right, it's not that, it's not—I just need a moment, that's all.'

*

Outside I sink down on the swing seat, lean my head against the soft cushions and look up at the glorious star-filled sky. For a long time after Frankie disappeared I was afraid of my bed, of those thoughts that came into my head when I lay down. Not thoughts, exactly—I don't think I had real thoughts in those dreadful days. I had images, and I shut them out, I pretended they weren't real. As you might say, my eyes were open, but their sense was closed. I pretended I believed what everyone else did, that Frankie had simply run away. I knew he hadn't, but if you pretend something long enough you can forget you are pretending, the story you tell yourself becomes almost real. Even now, this very moment, when I look up at those stars, for a moment I still feel the comfort they've always given me, a promise that somewhere in this world Frankie is looking up at them too.

Which is nonsense.

I know Frankie is dead.

Way down in that muddy region at the bottom of my mind I've known it since the night he disappeared. I knew it when I visited Currawong the first time and sat with old Ted Stormer in his living room, drinking orange cordial, the big chunk of ice rattling against the glass. I knew it every time I picked up the telephone and half expected to hear his voice, every time I went to the mailbox, imagining a letter from him might be inside. At St Finbar's, when I sneaked to the ledge where Frankie used to go and watch the sunrise, I knew what I was searching for in those cracks and hollows and murky pools: the button ripped from Etta's cassock, held for a moment, in Frankie's desperate hand.

It would have happened there, on the ledge, in that place my mother said was like a picture of the end. Frankie would have been watching the dark sea, the sickle moon bright above it, and Etta would have come creeping up on him. Frankie might have heard his footsteps, and turned—or perhaps he didn't, thinking it was me—and then it was too late. Etta's small determined paw thrust out and pushing, Frankie bewildered, unsteady on that pitted rock, grabbing at Etta, catching at that button which comes off in his hand and goes over with him. My teeth clench at that long astonished falling through the dark—and the end of it: the extinguishing of the lovely, lovely world. All these years when I've been too afraid to admit the meaning of those images: grey sand on a cassock, a missing button, a pitted ledge above the sea—I've let my lovely Frankie fall forever. *Fear is a kind of wickedness:* I've let him fall over and over, fall and fall and fall.

A breeze stirs the bushes in the garden, *ah ah*, it says, so gently, *ah ah ah*, the very same sound I heard that long-ago morning on the beach at Shoreham when Frankie's little ghost stood there next to me, watching the rosy sea.

The breeze drops. He's gone.

'Miri!' I call out. 'Miri!'

She comes.

*

Later on I go out and walk my old familiar route, the one Frankie took that night, the long way down Jellicoe Lane where he met Manda Sutton and everything flowed from there.

'I should have *told*,' I'd said to Miri. 'I should have told them at St Finbar's what I thought had happened.'

'But you didn't *know*. Not really.'

'Yes, I did.'

'In here, perhaps.' She tapped the front of my shirt, like she always does. Left side; she's got it right for good, now. 'But not in any way that people would accept, Tom. No one would have believed you. You were only a kid.'

'But later—when I wasn't a kid anymore.'

'No.' She shook her head. 'They still wouldn't have believed you.'

'You believe me.'

'That's because I know you. Because I've listened to you talking about Frankie for, oh—years and years. I can put all the bits together, but to anyone else, it's only supposition.' She threw out her hands. 'There was no proof, Tom. Not then, not now. No one really saw anything, not even you.'

'There was the sand—on Etta's cassock and his boots. The

only place you get that kind of sand is up there on that track to the ledge.'

She shrugged. 'He cleaned it off. It was only your word again. Anyway, the sand only meant he was there in that place, not that he did anything to Frankie. He could simply have been following him. Your word against his, again. And nothing more.'

We were both quiet for a minute. Then suddenly she flashed me her old smile. 'We could buy a gun and shoot him,' she said. 'We're ancient, no one will put us away.'

I smiled back at her sadly. I saw Frankie falling, falling, I saw Etta's little paws again, clasping and unclasping, washing and wringing—*Out, vile spot!*—and my eyes flicked towards the desk in the corner of the room. In the second drawer there's a letter opener, an innocent gift from a friend that I've never used. Its narrow wooden sheath is painted prettily with birds and flowers, inside the silvery blade of the stiletto gleams. I imagine strolling up to Etta at some function, sliding it swiftly through the smooth fabric of his soutane. It would be a silent death; I'm absolutely sure he'd make no sound. It could even be something he'd been waiting for, all these long, long years.

Suddenly I heard myself asking Miri, 'Do you think there might have been others?' My voice was so low I'm surprised she could hear; the question swam up from that cloudy region of my mind, surfacing unexpectedly, like a half rotted-body from the bottom of a lake. It's a question I've hidden from. Though once I did ask John Rushall—years after, as always.

'Remember?' I said. 'Back at St Finbar's, how you once told me Etta used to get these *downs* on some boys?'

'Yes,' he said quietly.

'What happened to them?'

'There were only two. One left. One was expelled.'

'Did you ever hear anything about them—I mean, later?'

'Well, Bob Geary, he went into law; Paul Cummings went to London, got a teaching job at University College, eventually.'

'So they were okay, then?'

'Sure, last time I heard. And what about your friend? That one who left, the one you were so worried about that time? You hear from him? What's he up to these days?'

'Ah—' I couldn't answer. I took to my heels and left him. I simply ran.

'Others?' echoed Miri.

'Other people Etta—' John Rushall's mild phrase slid softly from my tongue, 'had a down on.'

'Killed, you mean?' she said quite calmly. 'No, there wouldn't have been.'

'How—how do you know?'

'I'm quite sure of that, Tom.'

'Why? How can you be?'

'From all you've told me. About Etta. About his—love. Can you call it that?'

'No!'

'All the same, Frankie would have been the only one for him.'

The words bought a kind of desolation—to think that Etta and I also had this in common: that Frankie was the only one.

*

Now I stand in Jellicoe Lane beneath the cherry trees and think of the gifts Frankie left to me. He left me what knowledge I have of loving someone, a handful of memories and blessed images, little things that will never leave me: he had a way of turning his head to look at you, turning it slowly, nonchalantly, as if you were the last thing on his mind, and then all at once fixing you with those laughing, inky-blue eyes. Indigo. He left me that indigo richness, and his sense of the loveliness of the world; a hawk hovering, a sea like quilted silk, a flag snapping in the breeze—

A few years back I worked in a parish in the western suburbs of the city. It was a place where young people began their sex lives early and instead of the shapeless smocks respectability demanded when I was young, the pregnant girls wore bright clinging tee-shirts which emphasised the curved shape of their bellies. They walked proudly with their shoulders back and stood with a hand curved protectively round the unborn child. They looked wonderful and whenever I saw them I thought how Frankie would have stopped in his tracks and gazed—not out of lust or concupiscence, those damning words that sprang from our books like blows—but out of sheer amazed delight and gratitude for the loveliness of the world. 'Look, Frankie!' I'd whisper then. Anyone could have heard me—I didn't care.

'Look, Frankie.'

The moon is rising, and the air stirs with its perfume of damp grass and flowers and earth. These summer nights are so beautiful that sometimes for a moment I can almost feel that closeness of God I had when I was young, before St Finbar's, before Etta, before Frankie—that sense of His hand outstretched and loving, poised tenderly above my silly head.

Or perhaps it's Frankie up there, Frankie in his cloudless blue heaven, laughing, playing a little trick on me, his long brown fingers ruffling my sparse grey hair.

ABOUT THE AUTHOR

Judith Clarke was born in Sydney and educated at the University of New South Wales and the Australian National University in Canberra. She has worked as a teacher and librarian, and in adult education in Victoria and New South Wales.

Judith's novels include the multi-award-winning *Wolf on the Fold*, as well as *Friend of My Heart*, *Night Train*, *Starry Nights* and the very popular and funny *Al Capsella* series. *Kalpana's Dream* was an Honour Book in the 2005 Boston Globe–Horn Book Awards; *One Whole and Perfect Day* was a winner in the 2007 Queensland Premier's Literary Awards, shortlisted in the 2007 CBCA Book of the Year Awards and the NSW Premier's Literary Awards, and Honor Book in the American Literary Association's Michael L. Printz Awards for Excellence in Young Adult Literature 2008. *The Winds of Heaven* was an Honour Book in the 2010 CBCA Book of the Year Awards and shortlisted for the inaugural Prime Minister's Literary Award in 2010.

Judith's books have been published in the USA and Europe to high acclaim.

MORE WONDERFUL BOOKS BY JUDITH CLARKE

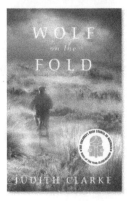